Becoming Alice

A Novel by Wayne Lasner

Writing is a socially acceptable form of schizophrenia.

E. L. Doctorow

Prologue

"Take my hand and walk with me."

"You are so beautiful."

"I am beautiful because of you. I look like you. We all do."

They walked through a lovely garden of freshly bloomed Tulips. The red flora went on to line a well-groomed winding path that appeared to be endless. All around them, trees gently swayed. Yet, there was no wind; not even a breeze. It was not warm nor cold; it just *was*.

"I feel like Dorothy in the Wizard of Oz, traveling the path leading to a final destination of peace and happiness."

The plush green grass softly bounced under her feet. It may not have been the 'Yellow brick road,' but she looked around for any strange characters.

"Where are we?"

She still sensed the gentle grip of the hand, but no longer recognized the face that was like a reflection in a mirror.

"Right now, we can be anywhere we want to be. We can do whatever we want, and we can say what comes to

mind. We write the story that controls everything around us."

"You keep saying 'we', like there are more of us. How do you define us? Who are 'we' really?"

"We share the same physical body, but our souls are unique. We are all part of you, and together we make a whole being. We watch out for each other."

Red tulips blanketed the surrounding hills, with glimpses of the plush grass fields peeking through. The deep blue sky had not a cloud to disrupt its solid pallet. They continued walking in silence for a while. She did not need to turn her head to know shadows, like spirits, followed.

They had conversation, but no words were spoken. She could not be sure if she asked the questions or answered them.

"Am I dreaming? Are we dead? Is this mystical place Heaven?"

They traversed the rolling hills of green grass and extravagant flora; time seemed to stand still. A darkening area to the left and far in front of them gained mass as they continued walking. A vision came to her, showing the blood filled waters of hell. She sensed the evil that could afford her much of the wild desires she occasionally dreamt of; and they seemed so real. The path they followed split; a choice had to be made. She now stared at herself, looking deep within.

The choice is a simple one, so she thought. The beauty lay beyond and to the right. The unknown to the left. In her head she heard,

"Have some fun, live a little. Take a chance."

Their hands no longer connected, her doppelganger floated off into the darkness. She felt as if part of her soul had split off, leaving her lonely and sad. She chose to follow the path to the right. The path surrounded by beautiful things and warm sunshine.

However, if they truly shared but one body, then which of the two paths, evil or good, had they really taken?

Chapter 1

West Hartford, CT

As dusk transitioned to night, a dense mist surrounded the jogger as she navigated one of the many curved paths of Westmoor Park. With summer finally approaching, the weather had already started to change. The now moderately warm days still lead to cooler, damp evenings. The jogger checked her wrist monitor, which indicated 3.2 miles. Finally, she had broken her three-mile record. With her adrenaline flowing, she decided to push a little more, raising the bar for the next days' run. She slowed to a fast-paced walk for a quick cool-down. As her breathing slowed down, so did the prancing clouds her breath formed as she exhaled. Above her, the mist took on an iridescent glow as the moon tried to peek through. She cherished the peace and quiet of the forest. Tonight, though, an uneasiness suddenly came over her. It seemed a bit too quiet. She had an eerie sense that someone was watching her. She held her breath and listened intently for a few seconds while she scrutinized her current surroundings for any signs of danger. Two days ago, while running this same path, she felt the same disturbing sensation. All had turned out safe then. She had no doubt it would now as well. Aloud, to the trees and peering wildlife, she said, "OK, here we go. For the world's record." The resilient jogger resumed her earlier pace.

The lights of the parking lot where her car sat alone amongst a hundred empty spaces glimmered through the sparse trees and mist. That was a sign for her to begin gradually slowing her pace. Her run for the night almost completed, she slowed down to a cooling off, fast-paced walk. From her right she heard rustling in the bushes. She reacted too slowly. Whatever hit her, knocked the wind out of her, causing a momentary loss of consciousness. At first, she thought the heavy breathing belonged to her. As it became louder and clearer, she realized it belonged to someone else. *Open your eyes!* Something heavy pushed on her face; she realized that her ability to breathe became more and more difficult; then impossible. As she desperately tried opening her eyes, panic ensued and unimaginable terror overcame her. The young woman tried to fight off her attacker, but to no avail.

The sun rose from the east announcing the arrival of morning. A park ranger, who had just started his solo shift, snatched a pack of cigarettes from his desk, "Time to make the rounds." He got into his jeep and drove from his office, located next to the information center, toward the main visitor parking lot. He at once noticed the one car parked at the far end, near where the trails began. He checked his wristwatch, noting the early hour of 6 AM. The park would not officially open for another two hours. A radio-check with dispatch showed no evidence that the car had been stolen or broken into. A closer inspection of the vehicle confirmed that all the doors were locked. On the front seat was a towel and a cooler bag. He thought, OK. These are items for a hiker or jogger. The ranger figured the person or persons belonging to this vehicle probably slipped in for an early hike. "Darn young fools. Always breaking the rules." Out of curiosity, the ranger placed the palm of his hand on the hood of the car, noting its coolness.

"This is Westmoor Ranger 23."

"Go ahead, ranger."

"We may have a lost hiker since overnight."

"Roger that. Will dispatch. Stand-by."

The ranger considered requesting an ambulance just in case there was a broken ankle, which happens with these crazy runners and the uneven terrain. Hypothermia is another possibility, but the night air was not all that cold yet. He knew that rescue teams in the area were limited, and could take a while to arrive. He decided to wait anyway. For all anyone knew, the unknown owner of the vehicle was sipping from a water bottle, and preparing to return at any moment.

The park ranger looked around for any approaching emergency or other vehicles. None were approaching. He leaned against his jeep, removed his hat and wiped his moist forehead. "Oh, well. I guess I've got time for a smoke."

Brooklyn, New York

Her handsome boyfriend did not call as promised this morning. His boss sent him to Hartford for an all-day meeting. He wanted her to come with him and coaxed her with things like, "You can lounge at the indoor pool or go for a massage. You can write all day and then we can play all night; on the company." He knew she had planned to go upstate. He also knew that she had to work, or risk her publisher dropping her as a client. Alice gave in, against her better judgment, and called him. She was hurt and disappointed. It rang four times before the voicemail picked up. "Damn it, Robert. Where are you?" She suspected him of cheating on her at least once during their relationship. He did a good job convincing her otherwise, but when he did things like this, it left her suspicious, and jealous. She grabbed her duffle bag and left her apartment. She wanted to get upstate by 9AM in order to get in a full day of writing. Alice had made this trip to her lake house so often, there were times she didn't even remember the whole drive upstate. Sometimes she would daydream. Fortunately, and she always thanked God, she managed to arrive at her sanctuary safe and sound. As she crossed the northbound Tappan Zee Bridge, she had one of those short daydreams. This time it was of Robert making love to a faceless woman. It looked like it might be her, but it

9

wasn't. It couldn't be; not like that. Alice chalked it up to one of her jealous fantasies; the kind she wrote about in her stories. She wondered what she would do if she actually caught her man with another woman. Aloud she said, "I'd kill him! I would strangle him dead." She took a deep breath and focused on her driving.

He's so handsome and sexy, he needs more than what you give him.

Alice struggled to remain calm. She dialed her car's satellite radio to a 90's alternative station and started singing along loud. Loud kept the obscure voices out of her head.

Chapter 2 - Crazy

Daylight rapidly transitioned to early evening dusk. She opened her eyes slowly, like an awakening after a drug-induced sleep. She held her breath in a moment of confusion. Then the blaring horn of some irate asshole followed by what must have been an obscene remark, made her cringe. Her window overlooked a busy 5th Avenue in the Gowanus section of Brooklyn. She thought it odd that her curtains were swaying, as if a gentle breeze flowed through their rolling folds. Eerie, actually, being that the window was securely shut. The sun had just set and street lamps slowly began to light. One by one, they popped on in a steady flow. At first, each had a dim glow, that slowly and steadily became brighter. A fire engine with bright red and white flashing lights rolled down the street below, disconcertingly silent. Then without warning, the loudest scream of a siren made her jump to her feet.

She looked around her simple, country style "A" frame home, her mind still in a state of confusion. The silence was so deafening that she still imagined the sirens blasting from below her Brooklyn apartment window. It seemed so real.

Her daydream now shattered by that loud and obscure imaginary disturbance, she sat up straight in her chair. Her hands, she realized were already on the keyboard, but nothing was typed on the screen. "Damn it!" Alice said it to herself and out-loud for any creature outside or in, that might have witnessed her dismay. Writers-Block hit her on day one. Earlier in the week, when she was home in Brooklyn, she had all kinds of interesting story lines running around in her head. Sometimes they were so intense, so clear in her mind; she swore someone else said them to her. Now, she diverted her soft gray eyes to the window. Apparently, her mind created better when distracted. Ideas came to her while driving in the car, or in the middle of the night; always when she was in no position to record the ideas. The sun hitting the window radiated intense heat. Even though she sat a good six feet from the window, her face felt flush; even so, she didn't mind. Alice watched as two young people kayaked past her property. The lake looked inviting. The warmth on her face made her forget that it was too early in the season; too cold to swim. "Perhaps in a few weeks." Alice said it to herself, and it sounded convincing. *I need to find my bathing suits.*

The sixteen-hundred square foot "A" frame house came back on the market two years ago. Evidently, there was little interest at that time, and the prior owners took it off the Multiple Listing Service listings for the winter. However, it still appeared in the local paper's listings. Alice had never considered purchasing a home, and for the life of her, could not figure out what made her, out of the blue, peruse the listings. It was as if a subconscious thought prompted her. Even weirder than that, as she re-read the listing, she could envision the house overlooking the lake as if she had been there, perhaps in another lifetime. She made an appointment with the owner, and drove up one Saturday morning. The front of the house faced onto a quiet winding road called "Lower Road East." "Love at first sight," is how she described it to Robert later that evening. Alice stood at the edge of the gravel driveway, staring at the house. The combination of soft brown wood framing and glass screamed, "Wide open view!" Even from where she stood, the glistening lake behind the house awed her. The panoramic backdrop peaked out from either side of the home. The current owners had excellent landscaping tastes. She could tell that a lot of love went into maintaining the property. She especially loved their use of large "Knock Out Rose" bushes for privacy along with other interesting foliage. The owner gave Alice a tour of the home and then brought her out to the lower landing. After admiring the gorgeous lake, Alice turned to face the rear of the house. The majority of the structure was all windows. She already noted from the interior tour that every room in the house had a view of the lake. She imagined sitting at her computer with the magnificent water view. Alice closed the deal that afternoon, and took possession three weeks later. Buying the lake house was one of the most exciting and happy times in her life, but remembering the odd circumstances leading her upstate in the first place, made her uneasy.

There had been other instances; of the odd memories. She wondered if she might be clairvoyant. Take, for instance, her boyfriend Robert. The night before she left for the lake house, she spent the evening with him. He suggested they have an intimate dinner at his place. Alice told him she wanted to get an early start for upstate in the morning. Robert, she thought, was one of the good guys; "a keeper." He understood her need for solitude when writing. More importantly, he accepted her quirkiness and sometimes scattered personality. He told her, "No problem, babe. We can hang out until you're ready to go home. Or, even better, why don't you spend the night and I'll drive you home early to get your things." *He really loves me.*

They managed to polish off two bottles of wine, then made out for a while on his couch. Her eyes remained closed as his touch sent waves of excitement throughout her body. Expressing his heated passion for her, *"Let's go into the bedroom. I want you! Like an animal." She whisked her hair from the front of her face, exposing her glistening forehead, "I want it hard and fast! And I hate when you call me Babe!"*

She pulled away from his passionate assault on her mouth.

"What?"

His lips still moist from her saliva, and his face flush, "What do you mean, what? I didn't say anything. My tongue was busy screwing the inside your mouth."

This too, made for an exceptional quality in her man. She had these moments from time to time where she imagined she heard things that were never said. She wondered if madness was slowly taking over her mind. Clairvoyance or insanity; either way, it excited her sexually. "Never mind me. I'm sorry." Alice took Robert's hand, and led him to the bedroom, where they slowly and methodically removed each other's clothing. He looked at her with love and passion as he gently eased her down to the bed. Her mind was at it again. A quick flash of Robert taking her from behind while holding her breasts firmly. The hallucination made her quiver. Suddenly, her vision became reality. Their sexual adventures were better than average, but more on the conservative side. Robert's sudden aggressiveness was a shocking, but a welcome surprise. His rhythmic movements sent her body into orgasmic heaven. She thought that perhaps she might pass out. This is when they would normally settle down, and Robert would hold her close and tell her how much he loved her. But, he was not done; continuing in full, increasingly rapid motion. "Robert! Stop. You're hurting me." She said it softly, informatively. "Not yet, Sarah!" Suddenly he went still inside her. His explosion filling her as his hand on her waist held her in a vice-like grip. Suddenly she orgasmed again. They both fell to the bed. Alice felt faint, and Robert's breathing sounded like that of a rabid dog. They lay silently together for a few minutes.

"Can you take me home now?"
"What?"
"You called me Sarah. Who's Sarah?"
"What? No I didn't. Your mind is playing tricks on you again."
"Do you have sex like that with her? And now you want it that way with me?"
"Babe, you surely seemed satisfied more than ever. I tried something new. I did it for you; for us."
"I hate it when you call me Babe!"
"No you don't!"
"Take me home."

I don't hate it; I love when you call me Babe. Who the hell is Sarah? Who the hell is Sarah? Haha, hehe.

The laughter echoed deep down in her mind as the ominous voice mocked Alice's frustration. She needed to clear her mind from the prior night. Maybe she was a little crazy. Robert deserved an apology; but, one would never be proffered.

A gentle breeze moved the warm morning air across her shoulders. It relaxed her. Alice walked to the end of her small dock, and sat on the edge. Her feet dangled in the water, making tiny ripples. To herself, she said, "It's so peaceful. I love it here." The reflections of homes across the lake in the water looked like a Winslow Homer watercolor painting. She tried concentrating on all the natural beauty surrounding her on this incredible morning. Her hallucinations, if that is what they were, still haunted her. Then it hit her. Clarity and inspiration derailed her quiet and reflective mood.

Alice's heart pounded as she waited for her laptop to boot. She opened her word processor and her fingers flew across the keyboard. She wrote, "Chapter One." These crazy thoughts and visions, many that seemed to come true, were her inspiration for a story. She would write about them and improvise with fictitious characters. The book would be a "whodunit;" but not in the classic sense.

Chapter 3 – Robert

The intense dreams he had overnight seemed so real, they left him confused when he awoke this morning. Dreams of lust and guilt fueled by his recent indiscretions plagued him for the past few weeks. One afternoon, back then, not five minutes after he got off the phone with his girlfriend, Alice, Satan knocked on his door.

Biblical stories tell of demons taking on human form, sometimes of people who are already familiar to us. In this case, a seductress of great beauty and cunning.

On that sinful day they met, she played him. Robert hung up the phone and walked out of his office, heading to the local Starbucks for a coffee. She magically appeared behind him on line. He felt her vibe. It was as if her aura took hold of him. When he turned around, his heart jumped. "Alice? What are you doing here?" She could tell his curiosity would lead to his excitement and willingness to play the game. "I had my hair done. Do you like it?" He loved her sweet smile. Today, however, it seemed different. "Sinister" is what came to mind, as he started his re-evaluation of the person he thought he knew so well. "You look incredible, Alice. I do like it." She touched his hand ever so lightly, sending sensual signals throughout his body. He had not felt this aroused by her for some time. Not since the early days when they first started dating. She commanded, "Call your office and tell them something came up that you need to deal with." Her persona changed overnight; it was exciting. She could have asked him to jump in front of a car on 6th Avenue and he would have.

They spent the afternoon making love in ways he never imagined. His mind raced. He sensed that something about her seemed out of place. Not only the new and exciting, downright unbelievable sex. It was as if she was another person entirely. Robert's heart raced as he lay next to her. Incredible passion flowed from her body. As they lay next to each other, flat on their backs, naked and still, she turned her head, facing him. He did the same in sync. He spoke first. "That was incredible. By far, the ultimate... I'm not complaining, but what just happened and who *are* you?" She did not smile, and her face remained expressionless. "Do you want to go again?" Without waiting for Robert to answer, she rolled over on top of him and started moving her body rhythmically over his. He almost forgot to breathe. "Oh my god, Alice. Yes!"

"Call me Sarah. Say it! Say my name."

"Sarah! Holy mother of...."

After twenty-eight months of dating, sleeping together, going to movies, hanging out at the beach, Robert though he knew everything about his woman. Now, he wondered how well he really knew this beautiful sexy woman lying next to him. She had always been stable, predictable and sensible. *Boring.* The relationship became serious quickly, even though their time spent together was sometimes sporadic. Alice wrote fiction novels. When she worked, she needed quiet time that spanned days or even weeks. When she took a hiatus from creating, or had an unexpected bout with "writer's block," Alice would attach herself to him like a magnet. At this moment, as he lay there, Robert had a sense that this would no longer be the case. Something snapped in her. Sure, he should be concerned, but, he liked the new version of his girlfriend.

"Have you ever cheated on me?" There was the question; he never considered she would find reason to ask him. Their relationship was tight. "No. Of course not. Why would you ask me that?" She stared at the ceiling, still expressionless. It was a bit disturbing. "Well, Rob; Imagine what I'd do if you did cheat on me." She made a whack gesture with her hand raised up towards the ceiling. She turned her head facing him. "I'm just messing with you. But, I'm serious about you calling me Sarah." Robert brushed her hair from in front of her face, and touched her lips gently with his finger. "Why?" "Cause that's my name silly." He looked at her questioningly; weird quickly became bizarre. "Wow, you think I'm her!" She took a deep breath. "You really think I'm Alice? I'm, Sarah. Alice is my drop dead gorgeous, but dreary, twin sister. She lives her fantasies through her writing; I live them in real life. Wouldn't you agree?" Rob had no idea how to react. He considered the possibility that his Alice had gone off the deep end. Then he supposed, perhaps she is messing with me, or perhaps researching for a book. Whatever was happening here, whoever she really is, he wanted more of the new version of her.

"I meant what I said about the cheating. She's my identical twin, so technically you're really not cheating. You can have sex with both of us. But, you can never tell her about us. She and I have not spoken in years. That's a story for another time. Don't *ever* try to bring us all together. If you do, it's over between us and probably with her as well."

Robert's mind raced as he considered the crazy but tantalizing situation this woman just presented to him.

Can I really do this? Have my cake and eat it too?

Chapter 4 – Dazed and Confused

The mesmerizing hum of the car's engine helped her to remain relaxed. Alice made a valiant attempt at opening her eyes, but they were so heavy. Her brain told her to go back to sleep, but something else made her want to open them. She sat back and took a slow, deep breath. *Open your eyes; Alice!* Her knee hit the steering wheel of her 2013 Camry. The brightness of the day burned as she obeyed the subconscious command and opened her eyes. *Crap! Not again.* This was not the first time Alice Beekman found herself sitting in her car early in the morning. In fact, she had this happen to her at all sorts of odd hours. She had no recollection of leaving her apartment, or the lake house when she was there working. Usually, she dismissed it with no reasoning why, and went about her day. She, on occasion, considered that she might be going a tad crazy.

Even on a *crazy* day, a good hot shower helped her find normalcy. Again, she noticed several red marks on her body and what looked like a hickey right at the spot where her neck joined her shoulder. This too, has happened to her with no explanation. *Must be somewhat of a reaction to something.* Today, her nipples hurt; almost as much as her head and back. Alice wrapped herself in a large soft bath towel and went into the bedroom. She looked out the window at her car. *No signs of an accident.* Her hair looked different; it was a little shorter. She actually liked the sassy look. *So weird, I must have been drunk last night and don't remember doing this to myself.*

He picked up after the second ring. "Hello. Robert here."

"Hey, sweetie. It's Alice."
"Oh, um. Hey, babe. What's up?"
"Nothing much. I just miss you."

The silence of his pause unnerved her. She felt like something was not quite right.

"I miss you too, babe. Is everything OK?"
"Yes. I'm fine. Did we hang out last night?"

Now Robert was confused. "Al, you're a hundred miles upstate. What are you asking?" Alice realized she sounded nuts. "Like I said, I'm missing you. I had intense dreams last night. I guess I'm a bit muddled these days. What did you do last night?" Again, silence.

"I hung out with the TV. Old episodes of M.A.S.H. were on one of the cable channels. I fell asleep early." Alice thought for a second. "Oh, because I called you at your office yesterday and they said you came in earlier, but left mid- morning." Robert stuttered. Guilt made him sweat. "Whoever you spoke with is mistaken. I ran out quickly for a coffee. I had a meeting as soon as I got back to the office." Alice sighed, "It's OK, sweetie. It doesn't matter. I promised my agent that I would try to write something today. The publisher is pushing for a shorter timeline for this one. I had better get started on it. I love you."

"Love you too, Alice. Bye."

Alice had no idea what prompted her to make up that fib about calling his office. She knew he was lying. She had no idea how; she just knew it.

Chapter 5 – Ordinary

Once again, Alice sat in front of her computer, staring at the LED screen. She closed her eyes for a second. She imagined Rob sitting alone in his office. She tried to analyze what was missing in their relationship. She mumbled to herself, "I love him. I'm certain he loves me too." Alice further rationalized in her mind that *the sex is, for the most part, good. Although, lacking a bit in the excitement department. We are an average couple. We are ordinary.* Ok. There it is, the truth revealed. Her mind wandered further as she fell into a deep sleep. Then came the dreams. Alice arrived at Robert's private office. The other employees stood outside their cubicles watching as she walked by them. She turned and smiled at them as she pushed open the partially closed office door and entered. Robert's coworkers looked on as her shapely figure disappeared as she slammed the door shut. She then proceeded to close the blinds covering his one large interior window. There were no spoken words needed as she mounted her man, who silently sat in his chair. She moved up and down on him faster and faster. Rob moaned softly, indicating his best effort to hold on longer. Alice kissed his lips. He held her hips firmly, guiding her in an up and down motion while slowing their tempo a bit. She looked over his shoulder at a mirror behind him on the wall. Her head appeared and disappeared as she moved up and down in a smooth rhythm. For one second, she swore the reflection the mirror returned was not hers. It looked like her, but not exactly. She sensed a presence of someone else. She and Rob were the only ones in that room, but somehow it felt like another woman was having sex along with them.

Alice's body quivered as she moaned loudly, so loudly that it woke her out of her daydream. Perspiration covered her entire body. She dreamed craziness again. In front of her, her computer screen beeped, indicating it would go into sleep mode in a minute. Words, lots of them, appeared on the screen. Surprised, but not so much so, as it had happened to her in the past; she had written some seriously good material. Alice laughed to herself, and then said aloud to know one, "I may be crazy, but I'm good." She accepted the fact that she had no idea how or when she had written so many pages.

Chapter 6 - Restless

She sat in a darkened room with her eyes closed. Soft music played in the background; it sounded like a never-ending Sting song. It did not matter that no radio or other music delivery device existed in the room. In her mind, it existed, and it was beautiful, and soothing. Occasionally, a honk of a car's horn could be heard, or the screeching of worn brakes. None of this disturbed her.

The mind is an interesting source of power. Sometimes you can manipulate it, and sometimes it controls you. Her mind, now at ease, in a rare moment where she had control. Daydreams are one of those things that follow suit for one to be able to direct the story line. They become a mix of fantasy and reality. We have to be awake for these events. In deep sleep, our subconscious is in control, and we have no influence in what plays in our minds. Tonight, however, she wants to envision peaceful things. She remembers images from when she was little. Her parents took her to a lake resort. Those good times were few and far between. Her acting out drove a once loving family apart. She manipulates her imagery and now sees a lake house with beautiful gardens and many tall trees. A warm, gentle glow emanates from the fireplace. From her window, she can look upon a tranquil lake. Its serenity; so inviting. Subtle ripples reflect themselves repeatedly on the calm dark water. Little star-like sparkles, glimmering from lights of adjacent properties remind her of a Fourth of July fireworks display. She smiles to herself; a rare event. These thoughts taunt her. *Oh, how I long for a reality like this.*

Now her eyes are wide open, but she is no longer directing the daydream. The room is so very dark, yet images are projected as if in a movie theater. In her mind's eye, she sees their eyes. They too are wide open. In the darkness, she can see the blood as it bathes her victims. They lay still, as their souls are sucked out of them. Her heart beats heavy as the craving grows deep within her. She is hungry from the images in her head and needs the real thing to satisfy that craving. She will need to take a life. Not tonight, though; tonight she has other things to do. She is well aware of the desire that will rise within her, making her anxious. The timing needs to be right. *Tomorrow; yes, tomorrow.*

A plan is in the making. A place for the hunt is chosen. She will need a prospect. Let the game begin! Random victims were never satisfying. Stalking a victim, getting to know a little about them, made the adventure all that more exciting. It also made for a more interesting story. She will wait in anticipation for the perfect moment.

Again, with eyes closed, more of the story will be written. Curiosity invades her selfless moment. All that blood she envisioned; it was not real. At least most of it. Her victims rarely had damage to their outer selves. She considered most of them beautiful. Beautiful creatures that needed to be set free. With the unrelenting compulsion to free her own soul, she found solace in the fact that her chosen ones had their own final release of anxiety. A newfound freedom.

With her eyes open once again, the merciless one sits back in her chair. Her laughter sounded ever so sinister. As if she had commanded a rewind of her thoughts, she thinks back to a few moments ago and has a revelation. Aloud and with anger in her voice she shouts, "A newfound freedom? Shit! They were terrified as they saw life leaving their own bodies. It felt damn good! To me."

Now, there is a truth to be told; let's pen that.

The author stared at the computer screen for a moment. Earlier in the day, chapter one had been completed. There was so much more to tell; so much more to create.

She continued writing her story.

Chapter 7 - Out for a stroll

One of the selling points of the lake house was the rights of passage around the lake. The last fifteen feet of beach leading down to the shoreline remained federally owned and protected. Homeowners had irrevocable privileges to cross from their property line to the permitted section of lake, where they had dock space. Each day, weather permitting, Alice would take a walk around the lake. Not the whole forty-three miles, but usually three or more. Sometimes she would go left, sometimes right. As she passed homes, residents would wave. Occasionally she would make short conversation or a quick howdy doo. Two brothers, one married, one single, owned a beautiful log cabin style home about twelve houses to the right. Last year, shortly after she purchased her lake house, she ran into the single brother as he was tying up his kayak. Alice asked how the water was. He expressed his thrill at being able to move rapidly across the glass-like water. They made small talk for a few minutes before the handsome young man asked her if she would like to come up for a cold drink. She noticed his brother standing on the house deck high above them. When he noticed Alice looking up at him, he waved. "So, what do you say?" Alice forgot the question. "Would you like to join me for a cold one?" *No way! The older brother is cute and married. He's safe. This one, you could be his older sister and he probably would fall in love before you finished the first beer. He just wants to do you. Look at his eyes. Always pay attention to the eyes.*

"Thanks. Maybe another time. I really have to get back now. See you around." She had misgivings afterwards about how she responded to the young man's invite. She knew it was rude. The commanding voice in her head often distracted Alice. The people closest to her had gotten used to it, and for the most part ignored her scattered attention span. Those who did not know her well, thought her lack of interest appeared a tad insolent.

Today, as she passed house "number twelve" as she named it, she waved when she saw the young man, without stopping.

The rustling in the bush, uphill from where she stood, startled her. Bears seldom came this close to inhabited homes, especially in season. However, it did sound like a large animal. Alice stood still and quiet. She controlled her breathing as best as possible. Now she only heard the soft rippling of the water behind her as it lapped the shoreline. Alice often thought of recording some of the outdoor sounds and playing them in the background while she wrote. She looked around at the house to her right and then the one to her left. No one around in either direction. If it was a bear, it could rip her apart and no one would hear. No one would help her. *Don't be a wimp! Get on with your walk.* Her mind spoke to her again. If common sense had a voice, there it was. Alice turned to the right to head home. She took one-step and without any further thought, turned back in the other direction. Aloud, she said, "Onward, girly!" Another loud crackle and the bushes started to shake. Panic should have ensued, but Alice kept on walking until the sound was directly behind her. She stopped, staying motionless for a moment. After taking a deep breath, she slowly turned around to see the cutest little deer standing in front of her. In a childlike voice Alice softly said, "Hi, Bambi. You are so cute. Where's your mama?" She took a step closer; the deer lifted his head, keeping its eyes focused on the human. Alice smiled; she felt the grin as if it had a mind of its own. She yelled as loud as she could, "SCAT! RRAH!" Her hands high up and waving, the animal's hair seemed to stand on end as it turned and sprinted back into the wooded area. Alice had no idea why she did such a mean thing. *I am such a crazy bitch sometimes. I really need therapy.*

Thankfully, her return home remained event free. She wrote for a few more hours and stopped when her stomach complained that it was hungry. She closed her eyes to rest them for a moment. She ran images of food through her mind, trying to decide what she wanted to eat. Burgers on the grill! She could all but smell them as if they were already cooking. Her imagination now had "Smell-A-Vision."

"I did it again." She said it aloud. A plate with remnants of ketchup and a lone fry sat next to her laptop. Alice noticed that there was a good amount more of written pages than before she dozed off, and this baffled her. Apparently, she had used her walk earlier today as inspiration for another chapter. Only, the deer lay dead; its throat viciously slashed. In her story, the main character had blood on his clothing. He had just fought with his girlfriend. He left the house angry and needed to blow off some steam. The deer suffered the unfortunate consequence of his need. Alice read the chapter a second time before deleting it. A chill ran across her shoulders as remorse over removing the horrible chapter, hit her unexpectedly.

The day had worn her out. Alice decided to watch the news, and try to fall asleep early. She needed to write more seriously and avoid trashy prose. Her mind switched gears, mid-thought; *No, trashy and violent content is good*.

The "News at Ten" came on as she closed her eyes.

Chapter 8 – On the Prowl

Westbound traffic on Interstate 84 moved as expected for this time of day. Getting out of the West Hartford business district slowed things down a bit. She figured that the return trip later this evening, or more likely early tomorrow morning, would be smoother going and take even less time. The exact destination still unknown, the killer checks her phone's navigation. The destination is set for Middletown, New York. She had no conscious idea what prompted her to head west. Except that, it was too risky to stay around town. Upstate New York had no alerts as far as she was aware. The cops at home were on high alert, which intensified her cravings even more. The frenzy hitting her town served two important issues. First and foremost, her physical and mental need. *Oh, how I long to take a life right under their noses. How exciting that would be.*

The speedometer read 65 MPH, as did the GPS speed indicator on her phone. The highway rolled along in front of her. The green signs flashed by in a blur until she saw her marker for Newburg. She was nearing her destination. She watched for the turn-off to US 6.

The scent of cinnamon filled the small two-bedroom town home. Vivian poured another glass of wine for her guest. The cinnamon scented candle on the dining room table flickered, making shadows jump on the surrounding walls. "I think I've had enough. Are you trying to get me drunk?" Marissa smiled shyly. "Cause it's working." Vivian put the bottle down and walked behind her friend. She ran her hands gently through Marissa's soft shoulder-length hair. "You are so sexy." Marissa took hold of Vivian's hands and pulled her close. Vivian rested her chin on Marissa's shoulder and kissed her cheek. "So, did it work?" Marissa asked, "What? The wine?" Vivian inhaled the coconut scent embedded in her friend's hair. "Your hair. The coconut infused with the cinnamon is making me lust for you." She slid her hands slowly down Marissa's arms. "The wine made me relaxed, but I didn't need it for any other reason. I'm already into you, Vivian. You should have realized that by now." Vivian thought back to the previous week. She and Marissa had started hanging our more often. Marissa was dating a guy she met in one of her college classes. The two young women knew each other from high school, and had only recently become socially friendly. After a few lunches and a dinner at Vivian's, they both knew there was a connection between them. Last week, Marissa called Vivian on the phone and asked if she could come to her place, lamenting that she had just broken up with her boyfriend. Now, here they were. This was the first intimate moment for the two of them. Vivian was not sure Marissa was ready, but she could not hold out any longer.

Marissa let go of Vivian's hands and twisted her body so they were now facing each other. "I didn't need the wine to know how much I like you, Vivian." She leaned in and kissed her friend. Vivian's lips were so soft. Just touching them with hers sent a tingle throughout her body. Their tongues met as they both stood up, Vivian now leading them both toward the bedroom. "Wait. It's really late, and I have a physics final at eight in the morning. Besides, we are moving too fast; we should slow things down." Vivian looked disappointed but then smiled. "You're right! The best things are worth waiting for. Are you up for drinks tomorrow? Maybe work on the next phase of our relationship?" "I'll be dreaming about it all night." "Don't get all worked up, save some of that fun for me."

"Will you walk me out?"

"Of course."

Two women emerged from a house holding hands and giggling. The killer walked toward them. She stopped and watched from a few feet away as the two passionately kissed. She heard the taller one say, "Call me after the exam. Good luck." The other female turned toward the killer, startling her. As they passed each other, they bumped shoulders. The young woman squeaked like a mouse. "Ooh, I'm so sorry." The killer said nothing; she just waved as if to say "no big deal" and kept walking.

Like a volcano ready to erupt, she needed to act soon. Her breathing already becoming rapid. The killer did an about-face, and picked up the pace, following behind the woman, who now started to cross the street. She apparently had a car parked close by. *Just a few more feet.* A street light is flickering on and off; mostly off. *Perfect.* Marissa dangles her keys and manages to chirp her alarm, signaling the door is unlocked. The killer quickens her pace in anticipation of taking her prey.

"Marissa! Wait!"

The other woman is running down the block. She stumbles, and almost falls. The killer turns back and walks on the sidewalk, back in the direction she just came from. She is frustrated and angry.

"You forgot your pocketbook, silly girl." "Oh my god, Vivian. Thank you. I guess you did a good job getting me sloshed. Do you want me to drive you back?" "No, I'll walk the whole block. Besides, I need a cool me down."

They kissed again for a moment. "OK, missy. That's enough for now, or I'll never leave."

"Bye." Vivian watched as her friend drove down the block. She was sad but so happy. She could not wait until the next day. She skipped a few times and then quickly strode home.

As Vivian crossed the street, she saw someone walking. She was sure it looked like the same woman she spotted earlier when she and Marissa had left the house. Vivian knew better, but walked down the street a few feet away from the woman, but studiously avoided making eye contact. As soon as Vivian was a few steps ahead, she noted the absence of any other people on the block and quickened her pace. She sensed something was seriously amiss.

The sudden impact to her back caused such agonizing pain that Vivian was sure a car had struck her from behind. Yet, she heard nothing. No car engine, no horn honking, no tires screeching. No sound at all. She fell face down. The concrete met her nose and cheek with such force that she momentarily stopped breathing. As she regained consciousness, she had no feeling in her body. Confusion overwhelmed her as she realized now she was on her back. The concrete beneath her rubbed her skin raw as her body was dragged across the payment. All Vivian saw were shadows of darkness and the dimming of what little light reflected above her; everything rapidly faded to black.

The killer looks around to make sure there were no witnesses. She manages to drag the lifeless body of her victim off to the side of the road, into high grass. She checks the street again before making her way back to her car. A dog barks; it is more of a yap. Down the street, she sees an old man walking his little dog. The killer checks her hoodie, making sure it obscures her face. She waits for the man and his dog to disappear around the corner before getting into her car.

There is a chill in the air; it is 2:10 AM. Another day has begun. The killer does not care; she is warm with satisfaction.   The events of the evening met her needs. It almost did not go well, but ended up so much more gratifying in the end.

She had beautiful eyes.

Chapter 9 – A Night on the Town

"Time to have fun, girl. I need action and I'm not hanging with that downstate loser, two hours away." Sarah checked her phone for the time, which showed eleven-fifteen. She continued to put on the final touches of her makeup. "Damn it, girl. You need to cut that 'Go natural' crap. Now I have to do all this work." She looked in the mirror for one final face check. "Not that we need makeup."

Sarah talked often to Alice. She asked and answered all the time. The fact that Alice only reacted to Sarah's outlandish behavior infuriated her. She needed to strike out and wake that girl up. While Sarah found great satisfaction in tormenting her alter ego, she also experienced loneliness. She wanted to share the fun with her. Share things like real twins should.

The drive into town took ten minutes. The unlit curved roads offered a good challenge. She hoped she would enjoy the drive home as much after drinking all night. *Hey, that's Alice's problem.* Sarah parked on the far lawn across from the bar. She heard the music blaring, even though her parking spot was at a good distance from the bar. Sarah checked her makeup one last time using the car's rearview mirror. She carefully stepped out of the car trying to keep her four-inch heels from sinking into the soft grassy earth. Laughter, then giggles, made her pause. She smiled to herself. *Some bitch is giving it up, and it's only a quarter to midnight.*

"Good evening, Miss Beekman. Nice to see you again." Sarah did not recognize the young man playing bouncer at the door. He pointed to himself with a sarcastic grin. "Jeff; I live on the lake, a-ways down from you." *OK, now I remember him. Alice's fantasy man.* "Oh, of course. Please, call me S… Alice. Nice to see you too. So; this is where you work?" She extended her hand as she realized she almost messed up her cover. Sarah needed to make a quick decision to play the part of her lame other self, or play the twin sister scenario. She already told him her name was Alice; better to stay with that. "Sorry about the other day, at the lake. I needed to get some work done; I have deadlines." His smile was so inviting. "Of course. You're a writer. Way cool. I looked you up on Amazon and read the opener to your last book. It sure peaked my interest. I'll have to read the rest of it. I may need to read it in private so as not to embarrass myself." He grinned boyishly from the awkwardness and quickly changed the subject. "So, are you here with anyone?" Sarah smiled and touched his chest softly. "No one in particular, at the moment. Will you look after me if I run into any problems?" From behind Jeff, a tall older guy with a mustache tapped Jeff's shoulder. "If you're done flirting, stamp her hand. There are other paying customers waiting to get in before the night is done." The boss man nodded to Sarah. His stone face said, "Move along, Miss." Sarah winked at Jeff and mouthed, "Later."

The music was an eclectic mix of country rock and new wave techno. Sarah looked around for the dance floor for a while before realizing there was none. Patrons danced in place wherever they were. Bodies grinding like in the 80's disco scene. She noted how young most of them were; many looked under-age and most appeared to be drunk, or stoned on something. Dancing her way to the bar, a few wandering hands attempted to grope her butt, and other parts of her body. She kept control, ignoring the obnoxiousness as she reached the bar. "Double whiskey, neat!" After a few rounds, she played the groping game herself. "Wahoo!" Her head twirled and her long flawless legs moved in perfect rhythm. Even with all the young and vivacious women flaunting themselves, Sarah, as Alice stood out amongst the crowd.

Sarah danced for what seemed like hours. Her head spinning from the combination of bad spirits and relentless motion. Fresh air seemed like a smart move. Sarah made her way toward the bar's exit door. She caught the lake neighbor watching her as she wiped her forehead with her sleeve. She made her way through the crowd. Refreshingly, cool air hit her as she passed Jeff. She moved close in on him, her face inches from his, "Still on the job? Too bad. I'd like to have a little fun with you, but I wouldn't want your boss man to get his knickers all in a bunch and take it out on you." Sarah winked, and then pouted. She sensed his stare even though her back was to him. She did not look back.

"Hey, can I bum one?" One of the two girls she addressed gave up a cigarette and offered Sarah a light. "Thanks." She took a walk to a small wooded area alongside the parking lot to relax, and cool off from her wildly animated dancing. As Sarah took a long drag on the cigarette, she heard what sounded like two guys laughing. They sounded like two idiots. First, she heard the snap of twigs breaking under their feet, followed by more giggling. She looked to her left to see the two not so young men staring at her and whispering to each other. Sarah, being Sarah, she sneered and said, "What are you two little girls looking at?" In her mind's eye, she saw Alice's imaginary dead and bloodied deer. It morphed into their two bodies lying on the forest floor. One of the guys took a few steps closer. His friend tried to grab his arm but he pulled away. "You're that writer bitch. I recognize you." His words slurred as he spoke. Sarah could not be sure if it was his speech or her alcohol impaired hearing. She took another drag on her cigarette and then flicked it in his direction. He said, "Bitch! You have really nice legs. Why don't you wrap them around my…" Sarah roared back at him, "What, your tiny little; oh forget it. You probably don't have one." The guy's face turned crimson. Fear hung over Alice as confusion and reality came crashing down upon her. She was alone in the woods. There were loud people noises and music off in the distance. In front of her, two young men. One, for sure, looked like he wanted to rape her. She was about to scream, but something stopped her. Sarah regained control. She envisioned biting the guy's hardware off and leaving him to drown in his own blood.

"Hey! What's going on here? Alice, you alright?" The other guy grabbed his friend with the big mouth and said, "Nothing's going on, just a misunderstanding. We're out of here. He pushed his friend in the direction of the bar and said without turning around, "Sorry, Miss." They both stumbled as they made their way out of the parking area. Jeff and his damsel in distress chuckled at the two buffoons.

"So, are you really worried my boss might hassle me? Or, are you a tease? Either works for me." Sarah looked at him as if she had something to say but no words came out. Then, before he could speak, she asked, "You got a cigarette?" Jeff shook his head, indicating no. "So, Alice; you're a smoker? Didn't have you pegged as one of them." "Why, Jeff? Is it not sexy?" He looked hungry, *for her*. "You are sexy. Smoking or not. In fact, you are smoking hot. It's just that..." Sarah poked Jeff in the chest with her finger. "You're not going to tell me you have a girlfriend are you? Cause..." "No. Of course not." Sarah took a step back. She had him right where she wanted him in her little game of nerves. "Oh shit." Her facial expression was intimidating. "Good-looking guy like you. Of course you don't. You're gay!" She said it with such conviction, and just loud enough to embarrass him in front of his peers. "No! I'm not gay." He noticed her sexy grin. He realized she was teasing him. "Check it out." Jeff pointed south. "Does that settle the issue?" Sarah thought, "Hmm, not gay, perhaps a little immature." Jeff continued. "What I meant to say is that you're so different here, tonight, than when we met at the lake." Sarah pushed him a bit more. "So you like girls and not guys? OK. But, all the nonbelievers over there can't see your neat little bulge." *It's really not little. Alice has no idea what she is missing out on, tonight. I'll take it for a test drive and maybe share with her later*. "Listen, mister. You had better kiss me quickly, and set them all *straight*." She laughed at her play on words. Jeff kissed her hard, backing Sarah against a tree. She grabbed him down south. Jeff lifted her skirt hoping she would uncage his beast and let him show her the real man in him.

"No! Not here." *Alice has a reputation to uphold.*

"Are you kidding? Holy…"

"Take me back to my place. And hurry."

"OK, Alice. You don't have to ask twice. Let's go."

Surrealism had a great effect on me because then I
realised that the imagery in my mind wasn't insanity.
Surrealism to me is reality.

John Lennon

Chapter 10 – There's a man in my bed!

Alice dreamt all night. The sexual fantasies that started a few weeks ago always involved Robert. Last night, her loyal, sensible boyfriend was far away and out of her mind. Even though it was only a dream, one that seemed to last all night, Jeff's lovemaking wore her out. Her whole body still quivered as she replayed it in her mind. Alice kept her eyes closed even though she awoke minutes ago. Her mind worked hard trying to decipher dream from reality. Sublime as her fantasy may have been, guilt shadowed it. Alice planned to drive back to the city to spend the rest of the weekend with Robert, as she did most weekends. He was the real deal, and she loved him. Sunlight hitting her face made her squint as she started to open her eyelids. She sat up and swung her feet onto the floor. Her nakedness bewildered her momentarily as she tried to remember her evening. She had no recollection of what she did after dinner or even undressing for bed. She had no memories of any of that. She never slept naked, alone.

"Hey, you."

Alice jumped up as she screamed. There, lying next to where she just slept, was a man. A man as naked as she. As her mind rapidly tried to interpret what likely happened, she realized it was the guy from Lake House #12.

"What the Fuck! How did you get in here? What did you do to me?" Nausea overcame Alice quickly. She pulled the sheet off the bed, frantically wrapping herself as she ran to the bathroom. The sink was the easiest, closest place to expel the poison that burned as it erupted out of her. Jeff sat on the edge of the bed putting on his pants as Alice came back into the bedroom. He looked as confused and scared as she did. "Alice, I don't understand. Why are you so freaked out?" Her glazed-over stare frightened him. She looked terrified. "We had an awesome time last night. At least, I thought so." In a trembling voice, she asked again, "How did you get into my house?" As she said it, she picked up her cell phone from the dresser to her right. "Get the FUCK out of here! I'm calling the police." Now panic took over his emotions. Jeff had no idea what happened to "the girl next door." "Wait! Alice, listen to me. Just wait a minute. I heard rumors you were a little crazy, but crazy is cool, so I thought. You came on to me. You seduced me and invited me back to your place. I guess you got so freaking drunk last night that you don't remember?" She saw sincerity in his face; he believed the crap he dished out. "I never went out last night! You're full of shit!" Her hands shook as she touched 9-1-1 and hit the little green send button. Jeff leaned over and picked up his shoes. He wanted to get out of there before any more lunacy occurred; and before the cops came. "Wait! Look at your hand. The stamp; it proves you were at the bar last night. Please, let's talk about what happened. I'll run through everything that I'm aware of that happened while you were there, and after; with us. Then you can call the cops if you still want." She still looked frightened. Jeff said, "If I raped you, if I was going to hurt you, would I be sitting here letting you call the police?"

"9-1-1 what is the emergency?"

Alice took a breath, "I'm so sorry. I hit the emergency button on my cell phone by mistake."

"Ma'am, is everything all right?"

Alice assured the dispatcher that she was fine, even though she was not completely sure of that.

Jeff, who had sat himself back down on the edge of the bed, started to stand up again. Alice put up her hand in a "Stop" motion. "Please, stay there. Away from me."

Alice listened in shocking disbelief as Jeff told as detailed a story as he could, of the previous night's events. He admitted that he thought about her a lot since they met that day along the edge of his lakefront property. He also told her that when she came on to him, a one-night stand with a drunk patron was not part of the plan. He already liked her, and hoped she really liked him. "So, when you asked me back to your place, it felt natural. I was sure that we both wanted the same thing. I fell asleep, happy to be lying next to you, and excited at the prospect of waking up and seeing your beautiful eyes." Alice wanted to buy into all the mushy romantic stuff he dished out. But, the whole story of how she ended up at the bar and then with him. None of it; not one bit stuck out in her memory. "I think I'm going nuts." Tears streamed down her cheek. Jeff stood up, expecting Alice to shout for him to stay away. He wanted to hold her. "Alice, can we get a cup of coffee and talk this out. Maybe I can help jog your memory." He held out his hand. She took it without hesitation. Her fear and anger suddenly gone. Neither considered the oddity of the next few moments.

They walked down to the kitchen together, hand in hand. They stopped in front of the sink where the coffee maker sat. He released his gentle grip on her hand but to his surprise, she held tight. Their eyes met, and she kissed him. His confused emotions did not stop him from kissing her back. As their lips parted, Alice said, "I don't have a clue as to what's happening to me, but I'm confident you can help me figure it out."

As they sat and drank coffee, they spoke about everything other than the events of the past twelve hours. Like friends.

"You know, I'm older than you?"
"Not by much."
"I have a boyfriend."
"I won't tell him; but you should."
"I don't know what is happening yet or what I should or will do."
"OK. I want to help you."

Kiss him! You know you really want to– as Alice. We can share. It's not the first time. But, that's my secret.

Jeff did notice that Alice seemed different from the sexy and pert woman at the bar. Today she was calm and sensible, soft and lovable. She now seemed vulnerable, and he found this version of her even sexier.

Sarah, deep down in Alice's subconscious, smiled. *Now we both have a secret.*

Chapter 11 – Mommy

Traffic, being lighter than usual, moved along smoothly as Linda Beekman read the sign for Winter Park. She exited Interstate 4 and headed toward her home. "Grandma, I'm hungry and I have to pee." At fifty-four, this grandmother of the cutest six-year-old never imagined she would end up doubling as a full-time mother. Raising Alice was not easy. Shortly after Alice's fourth birthday, her parents noticed a change in her behavior. She rapidly became forgetful and at times disruptive in social settings. She would do naughty things, and when confronted, would adamantly deny her involvement. What frightened her elders most was her sincere belief in those lies. After numerous visits with school principals and counselors, her parents finally took Alice to a psychiatrist for an evaluation. What the doctor told the Beekman parents horrified them. "Your daughter shows the signs of Dissociative Identity Disorder, or DID." Alice played in a room next to where her parents spoke with the doctor. A nurse sat with her and tried to distract her, offering to play a game. The wall between them had a one-way mirror. As they listened to the doctor, Linda Beekman kept staring at the window. Alice stood looking right into the mirror, right at her parents as if she could see them. The doctor explained further. "It appears your daughter has multiple personalities." Linda asked, timidly, "You mean like she has two different people in her little mind?" The horror displayed on Linda's face prompted the doctor to calm things down a bit, and continue before panic ensued. "At least two that we are aware of now. Your daughter will need a lot of attention and care. But with proper treatment and medication, we can hope to control it."

"So we can help her? Cure her?"

"No. I'm so sorry. We can help her, but sadly, there really is no cure. We can control the issue to some extent. She is very young so we do not fully understand yet how much one personality will dominate the other. I would like to admit her for a thirty-day evaluation. Then we will know more, and can decide on a treatment plan." Alice's parents were torn apart over leaving their little girl for such an extended period. They fought over it daily. Mr. Beekman was against leaving Alice even for one night. He told his wife, "You're her mother. You should deal with this!" Poor Alice cried every day, except when her alter persona took over. This petite, adorable little girl unnerved even the doctors. On the first day, and successive days thereafter, Alice would cry hysterically and then suddenly stop. She would focus on whoever was within reach. Her eyes would turn cold and her face appeared to turn into stone. She would rant like the star of the Exorcist movie, and insist on being sent home. Her behavior was so unnerving that one of the nursing assistants quit after the second day of Alice's confinement.

Years went by, along with many doctors. Linda remained in denial and refused when the last doctor agreed with several before him that for her own good, institutionalizing Alice was the best option. Alice, now seventeen, and faced with the threat of being locked away, miraculously self-corrected her personality swings. "It's really strange, mommy, but I'm doing really good lately." The lying stopped, and she was pleasant to be around again. Her grades improved, and she started reading books. Lots of them. After a few months, she started coming home from school late. She was a senior in high school and quite beautiful. Boys tried to date her at times, but rumors of her strange behavior scared most of the nice ones away. Her mom perceived the other boys, the wild ones, as undesirable, so she made sure they stayed away. Alice's dad left around her sixteenth birthday. He and Linda fought constantly over Alice and her treatment plan. He finally had enough. Linda was certain that his abandonment of them was the start of Alice's fall back to her other personality, the incarnation of Sarah. Whatever or whoever Alice split her time with previously, no longer existed.

Alice, who to her mom and doctors seemed under control, continued to do well in school and even won awards for creative writing. Her teachers raved of her incredible imagination, and her ability to put ideas on paper. They had no idea where her inspiration came from.

At seventeen and nearing graduation, Alice found herself suddenly pregnant. Her mother freaked out at her obvious lies about who she was with, and when. With tears in her eyes, she pleaded with her mom to believe her. "I swear, mommy. I never was with anyone. I'm a good girl. I have no idea how this happened. I must have been drugged and raped." Alice almost collapsed to the floor. Linda, all of sudden, realized that Alice was telling the truth. Things appeared so normal for so many months, that Linda had forgotton about the other personality. It must have dominated her mind and done horrible things to Alice and her body. "You have to get an abortion. It's the only way. You cannot bring a child into this world. Not now; not ever!" Alice looked up, her face so sad. "I know mommy, but," Alice froze; words stopped flowing from her mouth. Linda felt the chill as Sarah took over. "I'm going to have this baby. It's mine! I'll decide if it lives or dies." Linda had to think quick. "OK, but first tell me who you are. What do I call you?" Alice looked puzzled. Her mom fought off a wave of nausea, and tried to remain in control. "Mommy; it's me, Sarah. We may look alike, but we are so different. We're twins. Alice doesn't know it yet, but she wants this baby. I really don't. It's going to mess everything up! But Alice, she will be depressed and try something stupid like killing herself. I can save her. You need to stay out of my way. We can all coexist. You, me, Alice - and the little brat!"

Linda and Sarah had many more chats over the next few days. They worked out a plan for Linda to care for the baby. Sarah would convince Alice to move to New York after graduation and stay away from her mother and her daughter. Linda fell into the illusion, and at times forgot that Alice and Sarah were the same person. "Remember, Mommy, Alice is not aware of me, and we need to keep it that way. Things will get ugly if that changes."

Chapter 12 – Family

"Oh, that feels so good. You have the golden hands of a masseuse."

"A little lower."
"Yes; there. "
"Harder!"

Robert obeyed as his queen commanded. He rubbed her soft, beautiful back with conviction. Her muscles were tense. "I thought your argument for the lake house was for peace and tranquility. Didn't you tell me that writing freed your mind and soul?" Robert firmly pushed his fingers along her spine, stopping at the L5 level and applying more pressure to the area.

"Ah, a little lower."

That was Roberts cue....

Alice wanted to clear her mind of the last few days. At this moment, engaging in conversation was the last thing she wanted. After that most bewildering day with Jeff, she needed to reconfirm her emotional state. She needed Robert to help her do that. Earlier in the week, Alice made up an excuse, telling Robert she needed to catch up by working through the weekend. As Sunday afternoon came and went, guilt, accompanied by the need to make things right, caused her to call Robert and tell him she was on her way to see him.

Alice arrived at Robert's apartment a little after 7PM. As she walked down the bare walled entrance hall leading to the living room and kitchen area, she thought, *how bachelor boring*. She had the same urge to say something each time she visited him, but always refrained from making any remarks. *I know what you're thinking; pretty drab. Woman up and say something*. Alice tried disregarding the haunting voice in her head but then blurted out, "Hey, you. Why don't we hit Pottery Barn or Home Goods next week and get a few nice items for your entranceway? I mean something that says 'you'." Robert grinned; he looked bewildered from her remark but said, "Sure. Sounds like a plan."

To Robert's credit, he had a picnic blanket laid out on the living room floor. She noted the bottle of red wine and two long stemmed glasses. He neatly positioned two settings of folded napkins, chopsticks and white china plates, leaving just enough space for them to sit facing each other. Off to the side were several Chinese food containers. The pungent aroma stimulated her senses, making her hungry. They shared a sumptuous meal of Chinese takeout and finished the bottle of red wine.

"This is very romantic, Robert. I'm so impressed. Do you have any other surprises in store for me tonight?" Robert leaned in and kissed Alice gently on the lips. Her heart pounded, making her feel anxious. A whisper in her head, not quite the same as the voice that usually haunted her, said, *I think we are going to get some tonight, girl.* If she could see herself in a mirror, she was sure the person looking back would be her, smiling. Alice put her hand behind Rob's head and held him locked in the kiss. Robert pulled back for a moment and brushed a lock of hair away from in front of her face. "As a matter of fact, I do have another surprise for you."

"Lower. You have incredible hands." *He does; doesn't he?*

Alice did her best to ignore the subconscious voice, even though the intrusive words spoken created an uncanny sense that this sensual moment had played out at an earlier time. Even more disturbing, she had no recollection of this scenario occurring between them. At least not in the past weeks. Yet, it seemed as if they were together with his hands moving across her body just yesterday. *Oh, yes!* Robert understood that she now wanted a more intense stress relief plan. One that would work for both of them. Only a few days ago, he was with Alice's sister, Sarah. He somehow shed the guilt as soon as Alice took him in her arms. In some weird way, he sensed she knew about him and Sarah and she was accepting of it.

His hand slid down her back again, this time gliding over her backside and down the inside of her upper thigh. Her response was inviting, and he accepted. Robert had to be careful not to spark jealousy by changing up their usual lovemaking. He was amazed at how different the two sisters were in personality, and in the manner in which they enjoyed sex. He found equal pleasure in both. Sarah displayed an extremely exuberant attitude. Her *thick skin* would allow her to deal with any situation. Although, he feared what she would be like in an agitated, anger induced state. Alice, on the other hand, had a sensitive side that dominated her personality. She liked romance and tenderness. She would never intentionally hurt him or anyone. As for her sister, he would avoid turning his back on her.

"That was nice. I love you, baby."

"I love you too, Alice. I wish we could find more time to be together this week."

"Maybe next week. It's the book; you understand, don't you?"

"What about my office party Friday night? You promised to be there for me. My boss asked specifically if you would

63

attend with me. I'm fairly certain that he's going to offer me a promotion. At least I hope that's his plan." Rob paused with a little guilt of his own. "I'm sorry, babe, it's a long trip for you and I don't like you driving so far alone all the time. I can go solo." Alice said nothing. She knew he needed her by his side but she was exhausted and had so much work to do. In the back of her mind, the possibility that Jeff might have something to do with her staying upstate disturbed her. She said, "Thank you for understanding, babe. I'm sorry."

They lay in bed, Rob spooning her tightly. Even though Alice disappointed him about Friday night, he acted as if the discussion never happened. She somehow found a safe place in her confused world. "I want you to meet my family. I'm sure I never told you this, but, I have a daughter." Rob kissed the back of her head but said nothing. Alice never spoke of her family. He knew they existed from a frantic call he received a few months earlier from Linda. She had been trying to reach her daughter for days. She assumed Alice's alter ego had something to do with that. Linda kept her promise not to talk about Alice's, and Sarah's relationship. Sarah promised to play nice concerning Alice, Linda, and her daughter. The doctors also warned Linda that under certain stressful conditions, the alter ego could become the dominant one. In some cases, sending the "real person" away forever.

Rob wanted to talk about Alice's family with her. Telling her about the call from her mom would relieve some of the pressure. But he promised not to say anything, so he held onto that information for now. He kissed her again.

"That would be nice; I'd like to meet them."

Alice turned to face him. Rob thought he caught a hint of a smile. He said, "Wow, you have a daughter? She must be adorable; like her mother."

At that moment, Alice felt safe and secure lying there with him. "That's so sweet." The words came out without her even thinking about it. She hoped it didn't seem sarcastic. Rob did not appear to notice.

"This is so awesome; being here with you. I hate the fact that I have to get back and actually do some work." She kissed Rob on the cheek. He watched adoringly as she got dressed. "Alice, baby. Are you sure?" He gestured toward his "love machine." His eyes pleaded for reconsideration. She paused for a second, as if she was about to return to his bed. "So tempting. But, no. Besides, you have to work; don't you? Aren't you going to Hartford for that

65

meeting?" He looked disappointed. She said, "I'll call you later, stud."

Chapter 13 – Time to work

Although he adamantly denied the accusations, there was a competitive side to Jeff, especially when it came to his more successful older brother. Everything happened to the elder sibling first. From graduating college and getting a super job, to meeting the girl of his dreams and getting married. It all just flowed smoothly in perfect order. The two brothers got along for the most part. Lately, Jeff noticed a touch of despair in his brother. He knew work was good but his brother's marriage lacked something; excitement perhaps. Now it was his turn to get ahead in life. The job at the bar was temporary at best. Jeff's love of the hospitality business would eventually lead him to working for one of the big hotel chains. Maybe someday he would own his own B&B.

The younger Donovan brother found the woman who lived only a short distance down from his shared vacation home to be interesting; to say the least. He found himself thinking about her all the time. Their relationship, that of friendship or something more, definitely had an awkward beginning. Alice seemed distracted at times and definitely confused. The night they spent together captivated him. The sex was unbelievable. She fully participated in their lovemaking.

None of the other girls he dated, or bedded as one-night stands, could compare to Alice. She had a beauty that almost blinded him. Her flaky personality definitely presented him with an interesting, perhaps impossible challenge. When he first met her, she seemed shy. No. Not shy; reserved. After that one awesome night they spent together, reserved had been stricken from the dictionary. The next morning it was as if the Pod People had replaced Alice. Jeff should have been disturbed by the Dr. Jekyll and Mrs. Hyde syndrome that Alice unexpectedly displayed. It certainly was quite a quandary. Instead, it stirred up curiosity and excitement that he found sexually arousing as well. He also understood how frightened she was by whatever happened. He liked her; a lot. He wanted to spend more time with Alice to get to know her better. Jeff wanted be to there for her.

For several days after their sexual encounter, Jeff attempted to contact Alice. She refused to return his relentless calls. He even nonchalantly strolled past her house. Alice covertly peeked out her window. She wanted to call down to him, but something held her back. Jeff wondered if age had something to do with her reluctance, or perhaps she really did not believe he was innocent for what had happened between them. Then he brushed off both ideas as an absurd consideration. After all, he was only three years younger than she was. Even though they had spent hours talking out the events of the night before, he considered how unglued Alice became over not remembering the events of that night they were together.

She doesn't trust me.

Jeff hoped that the half day they spent working through the events leading up to and during that incident could get them past the uncomfortable part. When Alice left him that afternoon, she seemed more than OK and promised they would spend more time together to talk.

Alice sat back in her chair, taking a break from the long hours of writing. The night before, she had new dreams that inspired her. She woke a little after 4 AM and started working. Like all writers, she had to document her thoughts as soon as they popped into her head or they would dwindle away into forgotten memories. Around 7AM, with a hot cup of coffee, she reread the last few chapters. What she wrote, included dreams she had of her intimacy with Robert and her extreme sex with Jeff. Or, was the "hot and heavy" with Robert. She still tossed those memories back and forth; undecided which of them were reality, or fantasy. Either way, it made for great fiction. Alice smiled and said aloud to no one, "This is great stuff!"

Hunger hit Alice around 3PM. She had not taken any breaks since the morning; not even for lunch. At one point, she did pause, taking a moment to admire the beauty of the lake. Jeff stood there for just a moment. There must have been a light breeze as his reflection shimmered in the rippling water behind him. Alice was sure he looked up at her. She hoped the sun glare prevented him from seeing her looking back at him. Guilt still hung over her. She loved Robert and never intended to cheat on him. However, she liked Jeff a lot. Her mind kept bringing those perverse memories back. She craved more of him. More of Jeff. She wanted to experience her dreams of being with him like that, in a true state of awareness. She wanted the dream to be real.

Alice scanned the contents of her refrigerator, noting some interesting items. She grabbed a firm white onion from the vegetable bin. Its aroma was quite pungent, making her nose tingle. She nearly sneezed. "Hmm, this should be tasty." After chopping the onion into nice size chunks, she pulled out a cast iron pan and tossed them in. "OK. Some oil and a touch of butter and, a pinch of salt. This is going to be awesomely delicious." In the meat bin, she selected one of two ribeye steaks. She picked them up earlier in the week hoping that Jeff might join her for a romantic dinner. They needed to talk more, and she hoped or perhaps fantasized about him at her place. She continued talking to herself, "Too bad, I bet you would have enjoyed this meal. I would have liked the company, for a change."

I bet you would. You're not strong enough to handle two relationships. Leave that to me.

Alice stared down at her plate; steak and onions for one. She thought how lame her life really was. "I could too, handle both of them. It's lonely up here." Alice surprised herself at her unsolicited outburst. She had no idea why she said that. She considered guilt as a strong possibility. The things that excited her happened mostly in her mind. Real life consisted of work, and more work. Not that she didn't love her job. Every office worker or factory person probably dreamed of being a writer. Oh, the glory of putting pen to paper. If only they knew all the hard, tedious work behind the passion and intrigue of the story; all the frustration and fears of "writer's block." The author suffers the pain that allows the reader to experience things they cannot have in real life. *Sort of like me, and my crazy aberrations.* Loneliness came on quickly. Robert was two hours downstate, and probably tired. If she drove there now, they would end up watching TV, have goodnight sex and fall asleep. Jeff was two minutes down the hill and over a few houses. Her mind began to wander. *"Robert is mine; he's a real man with me, and a wimp with you. Now Jeff, he's good for a few more hot moments. Then we can be done with him. You should do him, or I will; again!"*

The phone rang, snapping Alice out of her freaky frame of mind. "Hello?" "Alice, it's Drew. How's it going?" Alice got hold of herself and replied, almost stuttering her first words. "Oh, shit. Hi, Drew. Sorry, I'm working, but I drifted into a daydream for a moment. I was talking to myself in my head when you called." She realized, that sounded crazy. "Well, sweetheart, that's what makes you such a remarkable writer. Keep talking to yourself and get it all down on paper, or computer. Or, whatever." Alice cleared her throat. "Actually, Drew. Miraculously, pages are being written, and it's going really well. I followed your suggestion to spice this one up, and I'm sure you'll like it. I hope to have a completed draft in the next few weeks." "That's good news, Alice. I didn't want to pressure you, but now I can tell you that the publisher has been putting pressure on me to do the same to you. How about sending me a few of the most recent chapters you've completed? Give me something to dangle in front of the publisher. Anyway, as far as the pressuring you bit; sounds like I'm off the hook. You made my day sweetheart."

Sweetheart? Really?
Actually, Alice; I wrote most of that 'awesome' stuff!

Alice said goodbye to her agent, feeling relieved that he was satisfied with her progress. With her eyes closed, she let her mind bring images of Jeff to the forefront. He held her arms above her head as he moved in and out of her. As he leaned in to kiss her on the lips, she pushed hard on his hands. They both rolled over, ending with her on top. The image of Jeff's fervent smile made her stir in her seat, bringing her close to an orgasm. Suddenly, a chill came over her. Her stomach hardened as if she was angry. Rage took hold; her eyes barely open, she grabbed a glass paperweight from the desk and threw it across the room. As fast as that anger came on, it was gone. *What, the hell just happened?*

Sarah's rage crawled up from the depths below, like Satan walking the earth. She had had enough. While she needed Alice, Sarah wanted to take the lead. Anyone who got in her way would pay dearly.

Chapter 14 – Town

"Good Morning, New York! I hope you-all are ready for a beautiful 'Hump Day' this Wednesday morning." The radio announcer's upbeat rhetoric helped Alice to awaken. She stretched and yawned, then swung her feet over the edge of the bed as she sat up and stretched one more time. Last evening, she had the most vivid dreams of her and Jeff, *and* of her and Rob. Like the dreams she experienced almost every night, the intensity left her unsure of the difference between reality and fantasy. Not all the dreams involved sex; although most of them did. Some of the "G" rated scripts reminisced of conflicts between her and Robert. Her suspicions that he was cheating, surely fueled her subconscious imagination. Then, there was the voice in her head. *It* even managed to get into her dreams. As if her paranoia over Robert's infidelity was not damaging enough, she feared the voices controlled her dreams. In her awakened state, that voice still haunted her.

Alice sat for a moment, letting her mind cleanse itself from the overnight baggage. Aloud, she told herself, "Today is a new day; I'm going to get some serious work accomplished." Her stomach grumbled. She rubbed it with the palm of her hand in a circular motion. That always seemed to calm her hunger, for the moment.

The coffee maker had "auto" turned on, making it ready for the first cup of morning coffee. Alice looked at the single cup brewer, then at the refrigerator. She decided to take the ten-minute drive into town. There were plenty of local stores to walk around after a hearty breakfast at the local diner. She headed back upstairs and swapped her sweats for jeans and a comfortable pullover top. After applying a modest amount of makeup and brushing her hair, she was ready. One last mirror check... *You look perfect. I prefer a little more on the eyes.*

Alice found a parking space on Broadway in front of Al's Hardware. Fortunately, municipality greed had not yet soiled this little town. There were discussions about installing Muni-meters, but the town council overruled it for a second year in a row. As a city girl accustomed to impossible parking situations everywhere, this little perk made her smile. Al Simpson, the hardware store's proprietor, waved from the doorway as Alice got out of her car. "Good morning, Miss Beekman." "Good morning Al. Enjoy this beautiful day." Al nodded and waved again.

In anticipation of a delicious breakfast, Alice hurried her way to the diner at the end of the block. She passed a few more stores, their owners just starting to put out their "Open" signs. A few of the merchants moved interesting articles they had for sale outside on the sidewalk. Some displayed signs that read, "Sale Today" or "Looking for something special? Please come in."

The alluring scent of steak and bacon hit Alice as she approached the end of the block. The old-fashioned diner's front door was open, allowing the delicious smells of breakfast to escape. She noticed the gold colored ribbon tying the doorknob to a hook in the side of the building. As Alice walked in, the owner who was seated on a bar stool at the register, greeted her. "Good morning, Alice. How are you on this fine day?" "Hi, Tony. I'm great, thank you. It smells so good outside and I'm famished. Was that intentional to draw hungry people into your place?" Tony laughed, "Counter, as usual?" "Yes. Please." Tony gestured toward the counter area. Alice found an open spot.

A young waitress walked over with a fresh cup of coffee. "Good morning, Miss Beekman. Here you go." She placed the steaming beverage on the counter in front of Alice. "Your usual? Bacon and Eggs?" "Good morning, Angela. It smelled so delicious as I walked in, I have to have the Steak and Eggs this morning." Angela smiled as she turned toward the register area. "Hey, Tony; your smell-a-vision advertising worked." She leaned on the counter; her face only a few inches from Alice's and quietly said, "You should have seen him this morning as we opened. He went crazy looking for the rubber doorstop. I told him, "Calm down, Tony. So it's lost. Big deal." She shook her head, and then smiled. She asked Alice, "How's the book going? I can't wait to read it. I love your writing style. Sometimes, I forget its just a story." Alice liked Angela. She was always sweet and friendly. The poor girl's mother passed away suddenly, last year. Angela was only seventeen, and still in high school. Her mom had worked at the diner too. Tony knew she needed money, especially with no dad or other family members in the picture. The dad abandoned his family when Angela was less than a year old, leaving her mom struggling to provide for her and her Angela. He offered Angela the job with flexible hours. Alice asked, "And, how are you doing with school? Are you managing OK?" Angela explained that she was barely making ends meet and sometimes had to pay her rent late. Alice felt sorry for her. She would leave a generous tip as she always did. "Anyway, Miss Beekman, I started community college; summer classes. Tony agreed to let me have the summer off so I can get a jump-start by taking three classes. I've been taking shifts on weekends and an occasional weekday here and there. Hopefully I can add a few more hours during the week in the fall." Alice told Angela how happy she was for her, and how impressed she was with Angela's determination.

"Thanks, Alice. Is it OK if I call you Alice? I'll be right back with your Steak and Eggs."

Poor, poor girl. Everybody has problems. Take you and me for instance. People think we're crazy. Well, actually you. They think you're crazy.

After finishing her most delicious and satisfying breakfast, and two cups of coffee, Alice wished Angela good luck and said goodbye to Tony. There were only a few people on the street, window shopping and running their errands. Alice checked her phone, noting the time as 10:43AM. She figured it was still early enough for a walk around town. The thrift shop had several interesting things. A few items on display had at one time, belonged to Alice. She donated them last summer. The thrift store ran as a not-for-profit, and supported several charities, including one for homeless children. Alice also enjoyed walking through the two antique shops in town.

After thirty minutes of browsing, and twice ignoring the voice telling her that *she never buys anything so why look,* Alice headed home to continue working on her book. Deadlines were approaching quickly, and the pressure on Alice was mounting. She had to get serious, and work every day for the rest of the week. She enjoyed her downtime, even if it lasted only a few hours.

Chapter 15 – I'll go, if you won't

Alice Beekman worked hard on her book over the next few days, finishing four more chapters. She reread and self-edited each one several times. After each read-through, her fascination increased for how real and how sensual her writing had become. Alice leaned back in her chair gazing out at the lake. She did this every so often, hoping to catch him looking up at her. At this point, and with all the crazy things that have happened, Alice began to doubt herself. There was no way for her to be sure, if seeing him that day last week was real; or simply, fantasy. Either way, she scanned the perimeter along the shoreline. To her disappointment, Jeff was nowhere to be seen. *You ignored his calls and made as if you did not see him when he was down there. What did you expect?*

Alice's cell phone chimed, announcing a call and snapping her back into the *now* zone. Her head spun as she reached over the top of her laptop for the phone. Rob made one last pitch to her. "Hey. I really miss you, Alice. How's the writing going?" They spoke for a while and then he asked. "So. Any chance you have reconsidered and can go with me tomorrow night? I'll drive up in the morning and hang while you work during the day. We can get dressed at the lake house and drive directly to the party.

I'll drive you back Sunday after breakfast." Alice wanted to say "yes." She glanced out the window at the lake. No, she wanted to stay and work. *Hmm, no sign of Jeff.* She started to say, "Sweetie, I." Her mind went blank and her head ached. She feared that she might be having a stroke. Then, darkness fell upon her.

"I wouldn't miss your party for anything. I'm sorry for appearing so selfish. I'll drive down myself, and meet you there. I'm so used to traveling back and forth, that I really don't mind." Rob was taken aback at her swift change of heart, but he was thrilled none-the-less. "Do you have something dressy at the lake house to impress my boss? As well as for me, too?" Rob thought that adding the last part of his question might have been out of character for him. Rob did not intend to make Alice uncomfortable with his remark. Actually, he hoped it would trigger a positive response. His onetime affair with her sister changed him. He had to be careful. He had to avoid repeating that surely dangerous liaison. Sarah had a huge grin that only she could see as she glanced in the Art Deco style mirror hanging on the wall to her left. "No. Why don't you go to my apartment? Pick up my black dress, the one with the slit that let's just a little leg peek through." Rob knew the one she wanted; he pictured it in his mind's eye. He thought; *a little leg? A lot, of those long sexy legs.* He responded with, "I like where you're going

with this. Go on, there must be more items on your list."
"And my matching black high heels." She heard Rob
starting to breathe heavier. "In the second drawer of my
closet dresser, you'll find an eclectic assortment of
panties and bras. You pick, any color, any flavor that gets
you thinking about our 'after party' party." Alice's
presumptuousness pleasantly surprised Rob. He found it
intoxicating. "Stockings, too. Find the sexiest ones that
match my outfit." Rob's heart banged away. Not only was
his request for *sexy* OK, it must have triggered something
of an arousal in her. *Don't stop now, babe*. Sarah paused
for a second. Rob found the silence intimidating. "No,
wait. Forget the black heels; I want to wear my new
pumps. The ones with four-inch heels. They have a stitch
of satin on the heel and lace up high above the ankle."
Rob envisioned the two of them together as he slowly,
methodically, unlaced her shoes. "There's also only one
very sexy laced black slip. You'll know which one when
you see it. You got all that?" Rob nodded to himself, his
imagination causing serious effects on his body. He said,
"This is like having phone sex. We definitely should do this
more often. Don't you need anything else?" Sarah sighed,
"Not without you being in the same room with me." Rob
often wondered why it took so long for women to get
ready for a night out. After this conversation, he had a
better appreciation of their efforts. He also wondered
about Alice's forwardness. It was unlike her, and more like

her sister. His mind flashed an image of last week. His carnal encounter with Sarah left an unforgettable imprint in his mind. After their heated union, she left his apartment abruptly, saying nothing about what had just happened between them. There was none of the bullshit like, "This was a mistake", or "You should call me." Alice's sister got dressed, kissed him passionately for a few seconds and walked out of his apartment. "Hey!" Sarah continued, "Are you paying attention? Earth to Robert! Book a room in the city. Wait for me to text you in the morning when I'm ready to leave here. You can reply with the hotel information." For ten minutes his quirkier than ever girlfriend barked orders. He had no complaint about those demands; he wanted more of the same, if she had more for him. Rob asked, "Alice?" She replied, "Robert? Does this not work for you?" Robert said, "Oh, it works for me. I really miss you, Alice." Rob calling her Alice frustrated Sarah. She wanted to scold him. She wanted to tell him that his renewed infatuation was with her, and not Alice. She calmed down quickly, not letting on how she felt. She said, "Good. Maybe I'll let you dress me before we go to the party; and undress me when we return to the hotel." Sarah's head started to throb. She had to fight off Alice's mighty effort to regain control. "Wait!" Rob asked, "Wait for what?" Sarah was not ready to end her time on the phone with Robert but she knew Alice would be relentless. "I have to get back to work, I'll see you tomorrow." Rob told her he loved her and said goodbye. She did not reply; she just hung up the phone. Frustration overcame him along with loneliness. He now could not get Alice out of his head. Before today, Sarah cluttered his sexual fantasies. Rob wanted Alice more than he could ever remember. Just *one more day*.

Alice sat there with her cell phone in her hand. Robert must have understood that she wanted to be there for him. He understood how tedious and long the drive was, and that she had a deadline.

Was he upset? I can't remember.

Chapter 16 – Detective Johnson

After a long afternoon in court, Detective Rhonda Johnson wanted one thing; a soak in her oversized Jacuzzi. Her husband of twelve years, now ex-husband, surprised her for their anniversary by having their master bath renovated. That was three years ago. They enjoyed many memorable moments together in that tub. Less than a year ago, her once stable and happy marriage ended in one single night. She, as much as anyone, understood the mid-life crisis men went through. Hell, women experienced the same frustrating times. The difference being that women were more devoted to working on their relationships. Men are weak and selfish and give up too easily. They fall prey to the first younger, pretty face willing to bed them. In a flash, it was over. Her marriage destroyed. Her man of fifteen years announced that he recently met someone. "It just happened. I'm truly sorry." He said all the expected things a man said out of guilt and selfishness. "He didn't mean for this to happen." "He fell in love." "He still loved her, but." Subconsciously, Rhonda still hoped her husband might see his mistake in judgment and return to her.

It took several months for the reality of her new life to sink in, and for her to come to terms with the fact that her husband would not be coming home. Before accepting that fact, she had become argumentative toward her coworkers and at times overly hostile to suspects during interrogations. Today, she got off easy. Some dirtbag sued her for unnecessary use of force during his arrest. Fortunately, a lengthy arrest record followed this guy, and the judge showed no sympathy for him. The judge dismissed the case against Detective Johnson with a warning given to her not to appear in his court again under similar circumstances.

Something about the scent of lavender relaxed her. Rhonda set the tub's timer to the max of fifteen minutes, and the water jets settings to "Soothing." She switched on her Bose bath radio and closed her eyes. The water swirled around her body as the bubbles tingled against her bare skin in a continuous soothing motion. *Now, this is delightful.*

She made it through the whole fifteen minutes without any interruptions, which was unusual. Rhonda wrapped herself in a large bath towel and patted herself dry. She reminisced back to when her husband would wrap the towel around her. He would hold her tightly in his arms, and kiss her while telling her how much he loved her. She missed the bastard.

"Hell, girl. You don't need this towel." She often spoke aloud to herself. She called it, self-therapy. Naked and proud, she strutted around the apartment feeling free. She glanced in the hallway mirror, *OK, maybe too much freedom*. Rhonda put on a soft robe and sat down with a glass of red wine. She opened the work folder that she had placed on the kitchen table when she got home earlier. The "Confidential File," as it was marked, had at least thirty pages in it. The first page, also marked confidential, along with a long-winded statement, had ADA Spencer's signature on it.

As she read the details of the file, a chill came over her. DNA evidence indicated that a two-time parolee named Edward Mullen, AKA "Scissor Hands," had molested an underage girl. He then carved her up and buried her body parts in a secluded wooded area in Central Park. A jogger discovered the body when his dog started pulling him and barking at something just off the path they were running along. As the jogger pulled his dog away, he noticed a hand partially exposed in the dirt and leaves. This case completely unnerved Rhonda. She had initially hoped his DNA would be a match to the serial killer in another case she was working. The creep swore it was not him, and that someone framed him for the crime. Other evidence confused things by indicating the possibility that there may have been others involved in the child's murder. With Detective Johnson's other case, the serial murders, all the evidence clearly indicated the crimes were committed by the same perpetrator. Additionally, burying the bodies was never the killers M.O. They also never found evidence of any forced sexual abuse in those cases. She checked her calendar confirming her meeting with ADA Spencer at 10AM in the morning to discuss the case. Rhonda was certain this particular murder case would be resolved, having nothing to do with her cold case.

Anne Spencer was a tough one. After her FBI husband mysteriously disappeared last year while working undercover, the ADA beat out depression and sadness by concentrating on her two children, and on her intense work schedule. There were not many details to explain what really happened, and Anne refrained from speaking about her own theories on the matter. Rhonda and Anne had worked on a few cases over the last two years. Anne was an impressive lawyer and certainly one you wanted on your side. During her short time working in New York City, she had rarely lost a conviction.

Reading a detailed crime brief after a relaxing bath, and a glass of wine, was not the best work strategy. Rhonda closed the file and made her way to the bedroom.

"Good night, world; tomorrow's another day. Good night, you bastard."

Chapter 17 – Into the City

Brrring, brrring.

 "Hey, handsome. I'm in the car, ready to head downstate. I hope you're well rested because I'm really hungry… for you."

"I hope you have a really good appetite. I already have what you asked for. I enjoyed the task."

"Ooh. Where?"

"Westin NYC, on 44th. I'll text the room number."

"I'm really hungry for you."

"Hurry; but be careful. And, don't text and drive."

Sarah had no idea how she did it. She seemed to be able to take control of this beautiful body almost at will. Alice, so far, did not seem to care or want to fight her way back. Sarah considered the consequences, thinking, "Things will get ugly should that change."

Traffic moved smoothly, allowing Sarah to make good time. She happily hummed an unfamiliar tune while tapping her foot and bobbing her head to the beat. As she exited the Palisades Parkway, her head started throbbing again. She sensed Alice fighting to regain control. "Oh, no you don't, Alice. Think, girl! Concentrate on him." She tried to imagine herself as Sarah with Robert. Anything that reinforced her, as her. The George Washington Bridge also had lighter than usual traffic. The city unfortunately, always made driving a chore. Her anticipation to see Robert kept her focused and in control. Sarah checked her watch, 11:12 AM. It only took her a little more than ninety-five minutes to reach the city.

The valet handed her a claim check. "Thank you, Miss. Enjoy your stay." She caught his admiring look as she walked away from her car.

Sarah checked her phone for text messages; there were none. Robert promised to text the room number to her before she arrived at the hotel. This annoyed her. She texted, "I'm here. What room?"

She waited in anticipation but no reply appeared on the screen. Sarah became anxious; anger began to build within her. *I need to calm down*. Sarah heard things in her head. "Damn it! No!" For a moment, her memory went blank. She lost all concept of time and space. Alice wanted to wake up. "NO! Not now!" A man standing by the elevators looked in her direction and then decided to mind his own business.

The phone buzzed, indicating a new text message had been received.

"Room 514. Left out of the elevator and about half way down the hall on the right."

For a about a minute, Alice stood in front of the garage elevator. She had no idea where she was or what the text message meant. She stood there forcing herself to slow her breathing and regain composure. Behind her, people started approaching. A little girl whined that she wanted to go swimming. The parents told her whatever she wanted to hear to quiet her down. She thought to herself, "Our parents did the same crap to us. They probably never cared enough to help us. It was easier to give in to our demands." Alice caught the dad glancing her way. With all the crazy noises in her head, she prayed that she had not uttered that last thought aloud.

Alice winced when the little girl accidently stepped on her toe. She immediately apologized. "I'm sorry." Her smile was adorable. "You are so cute. What's your name?" The little girl looked up with a radiant smile on her face and recited, "Dora." Dora's dad sported a fairly jaunty grin as well. Sarah wondered what thoughts crammed his Neanderthal brain. She wanted to ask him if he was done checking her out. *Control.* Alice, in control again for the moment said, "Well, hello Dora. That is a

91

beautiful name. Like Dora the Explorer." The little girl fidgeted in-place, "I love Dora the Explorer." "I bet you do. It is so nice to meet you, Dora; my name is Alice."

No one spoke on the ride up from the garage. The little girl smiled shyly and waved as the family exited at the lobby. Sarah shook her head. She told the child her name was Alice. She had no idea if she said Alice as part of scamming Robert, or Alice popped in for a quick "howdy do."

The elevator stopped at the fifth floor. None of the other passengers attempted to exit. Sarah glanced at the text message on her phone and got out of the elevator just as the doors started to close. "Suite 514, excellent!" Sarah found the room and knocked on the door. She felt empowered. So far, Robert obeyed every command. *Amazing how sex can control the male species. And, how much they want to be controlled.* "Open Sez Me."

Robert took her hand, and led her into the suite. She looked vulnerable, and perhaps confused. No spoken words were needed. He kissed her gently. She kissed him back, hard. When he spoke with Alice at the lake house, she agreed happily to join him for the weekend. He really missed her. The lips pressed against his own were not like hers. With his eyes closed, it very well could have been Sarah he now held close to him. He did notice her hair and how beautifully sexy she looked. Robert was certain that his lady would wow everyone at the party. He envisioned her in the outfit that he picked out for her. He had no doubt as to how sexy and refined she would appear. Nonetheless, the hair would need some fixing after their encounter this afternoon. On more than one occasion since meeting Sarah, Rob considered that Alice and her sister might very well be toying with him. Sharing him in some perverted, Patty Duke Show like, game. At some point, he would figure it all out. If that was the case, they are damn good. And, they look so much alike, even for identical twins. He loved Alice, and at the same time lusted for Sarah. He figured, if this situation is by definition insanity, then he was insane and OK with it. They may be having fun with him, and that's OK because he'd never been so turned on before. He would play the game as long as possible.

He was certain by the lovemaking, that the woman on top of him now, had to be Sarah. *You want to play? Let's play.* "Alice, baby; slow down. I want this moment to last longer; for you." The heat of the moment formed beads of perspiration on Sarah's face. Randomly they dropped on to Robert's; some reached his lips. The saltiness of the liquid drops elevated his level of excitement to a breaking point. Sarah realized this, crying out, "Oh, Yes!" Robert firmly pulled Sarah's hips down, against his own, and held her in place until she finished her explosive orgasm.

Robert kissed the woman next to him. His touch gently finding its way around her naked body. "That feels nice. Don't stop." Alice lay next to Rob saying nothing more for the moment. It happened again. Only this time, Robert lay next to her, and not Jeff. Confusion had become almost normal for her, and she accepted it for what it was. She had no idea where she was or how she got there. As for Robert, he needed to be careful. If the two sisters were playing with him, then he could milk his apparent ignorance of the situation. If they were not; if Sarah was pure evil, he had to be even more careful. He figured Alice and Sarah could not possibly share everything. He would cautiously ask questions that only Alice would know. If this was no game, and Sarah came instead of Alice, then Alice should be at the lake house. He would call her there, after the party.

Robert watched, as Alice got dressed. She moved slowly, methodically, as if she was not sure about what she was doing. As she laced up her sexy shoes, he considered making her take it all off and starting all over again. *And again.*

Alice stood up and shyly turned for Robert to zip her up. He gently guided her to turn and show off her outstanding outfit. "You look amazing. You are so incredibly beautiful." *Whichever sister you are.* Alice blushed. "Thank you. How did you know what dress to choose and what shoes went with it?" She seemed to blush even more, "Did you enjoy rummaging through my undergarments?" Now those two questions caught Robert off guard. Alice made him unsure of himself. He had no idea how to answer her question. Evidently, she did not remember the discussion from the other day. Or, it was Sarah he spoke with. Then somehow, Alice ended up coming downstate. He wondered what happened to Sarah if that was the case. The day began crazy and seemed to be headed, for insane. Maybe *he* was crazy. He took another good look at this beautiful, sexy lady. None of the thoughts in his head mattered at this point. She stood there, looking vulnerable and sexy. Rob extended his arm for her to take. "Shall we?"

Chapter 18 – Party Tonight!

Robert Evans and Alice Beekman walked into the Regency Room of the Grand Hyatt New York City Hotel, hand in hand, like the prom king and queen. They both looked like models; he out of a GQ magazine and she from the centerfold of a Victoria's Secret sexy dress edition. Rob kissed Alice and said, "Thank you for making this a perfect night. I love you Alice Beekman." She smiled, "I love you too, Robert." As she said it, he noticed a slight change in her demeanor. Her eyes seemed brighter, more alert. At first, she appeared a bit agitated, but he dismissed it as his own paranoia gone wild. Sarah *was* agitated. He told Alice that he loved her. She knew that when he says those words, they are for Alice and only her. That had to change. Sarah needed Robert to tell her, Sarah, that he loved her.

"I need a drink." Sarah took Robs hand and led him toward the bar. Flirting a smile at the bartender, "I'd like a dirty martini." She winked, "Very dirty, and three olives." Rob ordered a Jack and Ginger. He did not wink.

Drinks in hand, they clinked glasses. Robert looked at his girl in awe. They locked eyes, and at that moment, only the two of them existed. Alice smiled; she almost looked embarrassed as she felt a warmth flowing through her body. She so wanted to be anywhere but in that crowded room. The surprise of time and place no longer fazed her. She was home; last she remembered. In a blink of the eye, she is sitting with her guy at a bar; both of them dressed to kill. Alice immediately understood she was at Robert's company party in New York City. She should have been upset, confused at the very least. Amazingly, she was excited; like she was on an adventure, destination unknown. Robert caught a glimpse of his boss moving through the crowd and in their direction. He and Alice were having a special moment; he prayed someone would catch his boss's ear but that was not happening. "Robert, I'm so glad you were able to make it. That goes double for you, Alice; always a delight. You look ravishing this evening." Rob's boss extended his hand and graciously shook hers. Sarah flashed her sexy smile, "Thank you for inviting us, Mr. Stoltz." Her infectious smile having its way with the boss. "Mr. Stoltz is my father. Arnold, please." Sarah nodded and smiled again. Mr. Stoltz continued, "You know, Alice, your guy here is an ace recruiter. He has brought in more clients than any ten of our best people. We are very fortunate that he's on our team." Suddenly the boss became distracted, glancing away from her and Rob. "Cramer is here. Hmm Interesting, I don't see his partner. Do you mind, my dear, if I borrow Robert for a few moments?" Sarah smiled and nodded as she took a sip of her martini. "Of course not;

I'll schmooze and make some new friends." She glanced at Rob, not smiling. For some unclear reason, her fleeting stare made him nervous; perhaps jealous.

Rob and his boss spoke for a brief moment before walking over to greet the new client. Earlier, on the phone, Steven Cramer stated clearly that he wanted a top corporate executive to handle his account. "Steve, thank you so much for joining us tonight. I hope you're having a good time. Mr. Stoltz signaled to one of the waiters. Please, let me refresh your drink." Steve Cramer told the waiter, "Jack on ice. Thank you." The waiter said he would be back shortly with their drinks. Arnold wasted no time jumping right in with, "Well, Steve, as we discussed earlier, Cramer Industries will receive nothing but the best representation. Mr. Evans here will take care of your account personally. As a matter of fact, and Rob, you didn't hear this tonight; Rob will be promoted at the end of the month." He raised his glass to Robert, "To our new VP of Operations." They all raised their glasses. Steve Cramer addressed his two new business associates, "Well, then; we look forward to working with you, Mr. Evans." Rob raised his glass again, "Robert; please." He looked at his boss, trying to hold back his excitement, and then redirected his attention to the new client. "Well, with my new position, I'll have the means to ensure you get whatever you need to make this a winning venture for both our companies." Rob's boss offered to introduce Steve to some of the other key employees as well as other clients of his that might offer to share some value-added-resources. They walked off leaving Robert, drink in hand, to fend for himself. He wanted to avoid small talk with his coworkers, but felt compelled to say hello to a few people.

Rob headed toward the bar, stopping here and there to say hello to various employees and their wives, or significant others. He did not see Alice at the bar so he scanned the enormous ballroom for his stunning girlfriend. Alice seemed to have disappeared. The way she had been acting, nothing at this point would shock him. His mind raced; jealousy overcame him. "Hey!" The tap on his shoulder startled him. He turned abruptly to see his beauty queen arm and arm with his boss. *What the hell, Stoltz! I just left you!* Alice and Mr. Stoltz laughed together. Rob had to hold it together. "Hey." Stoltz patted Rob on the back, "Son, you got yourself a wild one here. I like her; she has spunk." His boss nodded, and with a sly grin strode off to greet his other guests. "I was looking for you, Alice." "As I, for you, Robert. I wish you could have seen your face. I'm not a lost puppy. I can take care of myself. Besides, I saw you looking for me but your lecherous boss latched on to my arm, distracting me. I think he touched my ass too; by accident. Maybe not."

Sarah enjoyed playing with Rob's psyche. She wanted to keep him on his toes. It also helped her to keep control of her; as Sarah. "Anyway, he told me the awesome news." Sarah positioned her hand on Rob's chest, his jacket hiding her suggestive movements. She brushed her finger over his chest and guided it a little further south towards his navel area. "Congratulations, my love." She kissed Rob and gently bit his lip while moving her hand upward on his chest. "I love this tie. Come with me to a secret place," she whispered. Sarah took Rob's hand and led him through the crowd of clients and coworkers. "Where are we going?" "Shush." The coat closet only had a few garments in it. Rob figured it was the employee's personal storage area. He asked, "How did you know about this?" "I have mystical powers. Let me show you." She had him under her spell. There was no turning back now. The jealousy and frustration of the evening, the mystique of Alice and her sister along with her assault on his body triggered a sexual rage in him. His reaction to her promiscuous come-on resulted in his own hard and fast assault on her. The pain she felt only drove her deeper into a sexual frenzy. Neither of them thought about their privacy.

Twenty minutes later, they exited the makeshift love nest. Both looked as if they went swimming in their clothing. "There's bathrooms right over there. I need a mirror. You need to fix your tie. And your hair." Sarah giggled. Rob wiped perspiration from his forehead, "You scoped out everything." He stopped, "Shit!" "What?" Rob pointed. "We have an audience." Several male and female hotel employees stood across the corridor looking embarrassed. Sarah giggled. Her outburst had an evil tone to it. "Who's next? We didn't use the sheets so, no need to change them." Rob grabbed her hand and pulled her away from them. "Come on!"

His appearance made more presentable after running a comb through his hair, Rob waited for Alice. Like all the miracles Alice had been producing lately, she looked incredible; better than before their romp in the coat room. He asked, as they walked back toward the banquet hall, "What was that all about?" "What, Robert. Did you not enjoy our little encounter?" "This is my career at stake; my promotion." The look on her face became scary, "You could have stopped me, but you didn't! I may be crazy but I clearly remember you ravishing my body quite willingly." Then she quietly said, "You've never turned me on so much. I'm still orgasming; like aftershocks. Actually," She turned, pulling him away from the party. "Let's go back to the hotel." Rob pulled his hand out of hers.

"Where is Alice? Why are you here with me? Does she even know about this party?" Defiantly, Sarah stated,

"My sister is a dud. She's busy writing and has no time for either one of us. She would never do with you what we just did; the way we did it." Her face looked really stressed. She continued. "You deserve more and I deserve you." As she said it, she realized that Sarah Beekman did not exist in the real world. Alice was in the forefront. The only way to remedy her situation would be to bury Alice's soul deep down; so far down, she could never come back. Sarah would then become Alice. Hell, *she* wrote most of the good material for her novel. Robert would be *hers*, and he could have his cake and eat it too; he would have Sarah, as Alice.

"I want to go back to our hotel. Hurry and find your boss. Make some excuse." Rob's face showed his discomfort with that idea, but she knew he would do as she commanded. "Tell him I'm not feeling well. Thank him for me. I'll wait in the lobby." Sarah turned away and headed for the lobby before Robert had a chance to say anything else. Rob thought, how cliché, "She's not well."

From behind him he heard her call out, "Don't keep me waiting, I might get lonely."

Chapter 19 – Get me out of here!

Alice finally realized the need to come to terms with, and accept, her apparent mental issues. She made a decision to avoid letting it destroy her life. She seemed to be lost more often, with missing moments in time. In each case though, she had weird memories that oddly made sense. She rationalized it as popping in and out of a dream state. Alice had no recollection of how she ended up at last night's company party in New York City. She found herself decked out in the midst of his coworkers, and then in a flash, here she was in a fancy hotel room, in bed with Robert. Later, after returning upstate to the lake house, she would have vivid memories of a wild night of drinking and sex; the events that filled in the blanked moments. Even stranger, her current writing would document it all under the alias of her fictional characters.

Alice let the hot water of the hotel shower run over her back. It was delightful; like tiny little fingers poking and massaging her. Relaxed, and enjoying the soothing moist heat, her mind began to wander. Images of a faceless man ravaging her body taunted her. Normally modest, she had the urge to summon Robert to join her. They had never showered together before, and as she fantasized, Robert became the faceless man; her body reacted. She suddenly ached for him. In her head she heard, "*Call him, you know you want him.*"

In a pleading voice, she called out to him, "Robert. I'm lonely."

The hotel bed had the firmest, yet most comfortable mattress. He had just dozed off when Sarah summoned him. The sheets were still crisp, even after hours of extreme lovemaking. His head pounded; the cost of over indulgent drinking. He sat up slowly, allowing himself to wake up and stretch. Sarah was not a woman of patience. When she called out a command, she expected a quick and fulfilling response. Since sex was the only major activity they shared, he shook off his needs, to appease hers. As he entered the steamy shower, her beautiful glistening body remedied anything that still ailed him. Somehow, Rob sensed that this was a time for slow seductive lovemaking. Tears flowed as he embraced her. The shower hid her distress. Alice's body quivered in rhythm with his. Rob sucked gently on her earlobe followed by a gentle kiss to her lips. As he worked his way down her neck, he told her, "You drive me insane, Sarah. I'm crazy for you." Alice said nothing at first. As he started to climax, she moaned loudly, then pushed him away.

"What?"

"You called me Sarah; again."

Rob was dumbfounded. "Are you kidding? Are we playing this game again?"

Robert grabbed her firmly and turned her so her back was to him. He held her arms above her head, against the moist shower wall as he forced himself upon her. She tried to resist his assault, but it seemed futile. While angst outwardly dominated her emotions, something deep inside her found Robert's aggressiveness physically satisfying. She said nothing as she gave in and let him satisfy his impetuous act of lust.

Rob reached around Alice, turning off the shower and started to say, "Wow. That was..." Still facing away from him, Alice reached behind her and pushed Robert away as he tried to kiss the back of her neck. The steam rushed out as he slid the shower door open, creating a dense fog in the bathroom.

Still wrapped in the plush hotel supplied robe, Alice started throwing her belongings into her overnight bag that was sitting on a valet stand. She had no recollection of driving downstate, let alone packing that bag. Yet, she had become accustomed to accepting the oddity of her apparent memory lapses.

"I'm leaving."

Rob pleaded for her to stay. He even "played the game" and called her Alice. At 3 AM, she crossed the George Washington Bridge on her journey back upstate. Melancholy and teary eyed, Alice drove at a moderate speed. She had stormed out of the hotel room hurt and angry. This was not like her. When she and Rob fought in the past, they always talked it out. Alice feared an evil force was in play, seeking to destroy their relationship. Alice arrived home at 5:15 AM.

The sun slowly rose in the east, and was just above the rim of the lake. Alice leaned against her car, taking in the peacefulness of its beauty. It was Sunday; her favorite day of the week. Saturday was a vague memory. Some of what she remembered, she wanted to forget. She considered the fact that *crazy* had all but taken over her state of mind. But, Rob seemed to be taking advantage of the circumstances. She pondered for a moment that his inconsiderate actions might be intentional. *Maybe he is bored with me. Perhaps I'm boring.*

Chapter 20 – Friends?

The events of the weekend all but wore Alice out. She sensed betrayal; only she had no idea why, or by whom. Being crazy, for lack of any other appropriate term, worked for her. It allowed her to accept the blacked out periods. She even found herself being OK with waking up in odd places, or with people, she had no plans to be with in that way. Robert, on the other hand, angered her. He was not compassionate to her fragile state of mind. He even appeared to enjoy it at times. He did things out of character for him and coerced her to comply. Only, she cannot remember how he did that. He never hurt her; at least not that she was aware of. It was some sort of perversion that he brought into their relationship. She was frightened of him, and even more so, that during her blacked out periods, she must have enjoyed the game he played with her.

Jeff, on the other hand, was the one constant. He seemed to accept her strange behavior. He even suggested she let him help her figure out what was happening to her. Alice did not fully understand why, but she trusted Jeff.

Just outside her large picture window, a hummingbird fluttered among the colorful flowers.

"Hello, cutie." As if the feathered helicopter heard her, it bounced to the other side of the floral arrangement, closer to the window. Again, to herself, Alice made a plan. "It's such a beautiful day. A walk around the lake seems in order."

Alice traversed the zigzagging wooden stairs and stepped onto the rocky edge of the lake. Her exact destination pre-programmed in her head. Her heart pounded in anticipation. *What if he's not there?* Each house had a uniqueness about it. Alice loved looking and comparing. For now, her observations allowed her to clear her mind and calm herself. *Just one more house.* She took a deep cleansing breath and exhaled slowly. The birds chirped their songs, and little chipmunks scurried in the leaves uphill from her. There were no heavy footsteps, nothing scary today. There were no deer in sight.

House #12, the one way up on the hill, looked intimidating. It was one of the larger homes on the lake. It also had the longest set of stairs leading from the lakeside to the lower and upper levels of the home. She stood facing the house, hoping to see him staring back at her, perhaps waving to her. Her nose detected the scent of burnt wood. She looked around and saw the source. Evidently, someone had enjoyed an evening by the fire. She imagined herself sitting in one of the Adirondack chairs sipping delicious wine. The fire cast shadows on Jeff as he raised his glass. His young face, his mouth so inviting.

"Hey there! Up here, Alice." Her daydream of Jeff broken by reality. There he was, waving; to her. She smiled and waved back. Jeff pointed up toward the sky with his index finger and raised his other hand, which held a very appealing bottle of beer. Alice gestured her wish to join him and started walking up the rocky knoll. The zigzag of his stairs definitely required a bit more stamina than hers did. "Whew, I thought mine were tough to climb." Jeff already had an ice-cold beer uncapped and waiting for her. "One cold brewski for the pretty lady."

Without hesitation, Jeff started with, "About the other night, um morning." Alice stopped him cold. "It's in the past; let's start over, fresh." She blushed as she ignored her own advice, "Was it... I mean was I...?" "Listen Alice; that night was incredible and you, well we, really enjoyed being together. I don't mean to make you uncomfortable, but you did ask." Alice, still blushing, said, "I'm an idiot. I don't remember, but then again, I do. I believe you; that we had a good time. It would be worse if it was awful; our being together." "In truth, Alice, you've been on my mind every moment since that night. I know that you have no memory of what happened between us, but at the time, it felt right." He took her hand. "We can

109

start over, but I have to be honest; I want to be with you. I've fallen for you; and you're not crazy. Something else is going on here. We'll figure it out, together." Alice's heart pounded. Her face went flush. *Kiss him! You know you want to.* Despite her impulse feelings, she held back, trying to keep everything under control. She became lightheaded. *Jump his bones! You know you want to! Remember how good it was the other night. Seduce him. He desires you.* There were those crazy thoughts again. The voice in her head. During her momentary lapse from reality, Jeff had moved closer. He looked like a little puppy waiting for his master to pat his head. "Oh, my. I'm so sorry, Jeff. It, it's happening again." Her left hand was on his thigh and her right held his hand firmly, gently pulling him closer. She removed both slowly. "I'm so embarrassed."

Sarah attempted to intervene in Alice's moment with Jeff. She tried to impose her evil desires on her soulmate. Alice subconsciously fought back and kept control of her actions and her awareness.

Sarah's anger churned in Alice's belly. Alice supposed she had agita.

This Jeff guy is going to ruin everything. Sure, we want to have a little fun with him. But, feelings for him? No way! We need Robert. Robert is clueless and easily duped. We can control him. We can share him. He certainly likes having it both ways. We can do this until only one of us is left to exist. That is going to be me, as you, Alice dear. Jeff has to go!

"Earth to Alice." Alice was deep in thought again, but had no recollection of the subject matter. She looked perplexed, making Jeff a little uncomfortable. Then she smiled and commanded him, "Kiss me! Quick, while I still have my wits about me, and the courage." At first, they kissed like the first time at senior prom. Then the fire was lit. Alice pulled away slowly. "I have a boyfriend." After a few seconds pause, she added, "His name is Robert." She paused for another second. "I'm just saying." Jeff looked like he wanted to say something but could not. Alice continued. "If I felt like this the other night, then I understand why we did what we did." Her heart pounded, she was anxious. Jeff took her hand and pulled her to her feet. "Let's take a walk; slow things down a bit. We have plenty of time to talk this out."

The lake looked like a mirror, reflecting the shoreline and its adjacent tree lined ridges. The two of them had walked a good distance. The lake homes on this part of the shore were spread apart more than most. It was quiet and secluded. It made for a romantic moment. Being with Jeff made her happy. "I love it here; it's so beautiful and peaceful." They held hands as they leisurely walked at the water's edge. Jeff stopped and took Alice's other hand. "You are beautiful; and sexy. You have been on my mind non-stop. I'm so glad you came by today." He kissed her right hand, still holding both. Alice asked, "Doesn't it bother you that I'm older than you?" Jeff laughed the kind of laugh that says "That's ridiculous." He pulled her close. "What, by two years? You're not old. Besides, older women are sexier and more experienced. Are you?" "Am I what?" She laughed from embarrassment. "Experienced." The image in her mind of her sleeping with Jeff and not remembering it unnerved her. She grew anxious and appeared upset. "You see me as a slut, don't you? What happened between us the other day; that was a onetime only event. It never happened before; not to me. I would have never done that, if subconsciously, I didn't want to be with you!" *Yes, you would have, or should I say, I would have.* "Shut Up!"

Jeff only had seconds to ponder his next move. "I didn't say anything, Alice."

"Alice doesn't live here anymore! She can't come out to play."

Her face twisted like in the movie "The Exorcist," only her face turned red, not green.

"We should head back; I'll make us tea and we can relax and talk." This time she took his hands and pulled him close. Sarah kissed him. She whispered, "I'm sorry." Jeff's mind said, "It's OK, Alice," but, no words left his lips. Sara began undressing him. As she undid his shirt, she caressed his chest with moist lips. She continued the process, removing the rest of his clothing. Jeff attempted to reciprocate but Sarah pushed him down on his back. The stone beneath him stung his bare skin. Her intense look told him to lay there and wait for her. She quickly removed her clothing, tossing each garment into a pile next to his. The sun reflecting off the water's edge made her glow like a goddess. Sarah was in another one of her sexual frenzies. It turned Jeff on in ways he could never express. This side of her frightened him, adding to his sexual ecstasy. "What about the neighbors?" She stopped for a second; she looked very serious. "Fuck the neighbors! What about Robert? What do you think he would do to you if he caught us?" The bewildering moment they were having just got weirder. Jeff gently pushed Alice aside. Sarah was clearly in control, "Oh no you don't!"

Chapter 21 – Reunited

A flurry of detectives and beat cops ran around the squad room, a place Detective Rhonda Johnson called her second home. It was a routine Monday for most of them. Unfortunately, Detective Rhonda Johnson's day would be anything but routine. She was holding a fax from a detective working out of the West Hartford Police Department on Raymond Road. Three years earlier, she and Detective Bill Reynolds had shared a homicide case. The *unsub*, short for unknown subject of an investigation, was thought to be a serial killer working randomly between New York and Connecticut. Their joint task force failed to apprehend anyone for the two murders in Hartford and the one in upper Manhattan. DNA taken from all three crime scenes, as well as the M.O. all matched. In each case, the New York woman and the two men in different suburbs of Hartford were found in a lake or small river. In all three cases, evidence indicated physical abuse, sometimes brutal, but no sexual contact. In each case, the coroner confirmed death by strangulation. The bodies were discovered at or near the site of the attack. The FBI, along with Crime Scene investigator profilers from both teams argued whether the *unsub* was male or female. After an intense fourteen-month long investigation, the case ended up going cold.

It was an embarrassing political debacle. After almost three years, the case had been all but forgotten. It was assumed that the killer had been arrested on another crime and his DNA had not found its way into the system for some unknown reason. Or, more likely, drugs or an accident killed him; or her. Now, as Detective Johnson read the communication that flooded all police jurisdictions in the tristate region. A chill came over her that made her shiver.

Her desk phone rang just as she put the disturbing communication down on top of an already overabundant stack of case files. "Rhonda? Bill Reynolds." Her stomach churned acid. "Detective Reynolds, Bill, how are you?" They chatted for a while about this and that, and caught up on the past three years. Detective Reynolds said, "So, I guess we're reuniting the task force again. Another body turned up here in West Hartford. She was found Tuesday." Rhonda said, "Interesting that you only got word of this today." Detective Bill Reynolds continued. "It only came across my desk after the crime scene investigators on the case ran DNA found at the scene. A match to an unknown suspect from other cold cases popped up, hence the call to me. I have no idea why it took so long to get to my desk. Turns out, this one was a young female jogger. She was found in Westmoor Park. Unlike the earlier murders, our Vic was found on dry ground. The assault took place far from any lakes or ponds. In any event, the M.O. may have changed a bit but DNA found at the scene suggests our serial killer is back in business." Rhonda asked, "So, it looks like he might have been incarcerated and the system screwed up his processing somehow, or he fled the country for a while. What's your take on this, Bill?" "My profiler is fairly certain the guy went cold on his own, perhaps satisfied with the three kills. Perhaps he met someone who calmed his needs. The consensus here is that something must have triggered the killer instinct again, perhaps a failed love interest." Rhonda sighed, "That makes sense." "There's something else, Rhonda. If the pattern holds true, you should be on the lookout for a body." They spoke for a while longer and agreed to reconvene later in the week as a group via video conference.

Rhonda thought, "OK. There goes my quiet week; month." Then out loud she said, "Freaking whole year!" She started jotting notes and formulating her own plan to search all murders across the tri-state region. She also texted her team of detectives, announcing a meeting for first thing the following morning. Next, she headed across the squad room to talk with her commanding officer. Rhonda knocked, taking notice of the new plaque "Captain Joe Delgado." She pushed the partially open door and walked in, not waiting for an invitation. Her captain did not look up from whatever he was reading. She often thought he had a unique sense, like eyes in the back of his head. "Why are you here so late?" Rhonda replied as if she had not heard what he just said, "Nice brass plaque. I see you finally got your name on the door." He looked up, and as his eyes met hers he said, "What's on your mind, Johnson? Whatever it is, it better not rile-up my hemorrhoids."

After repeating the details of her conversation with Detective Reynolds from the West Hartford Police Department, she brought her captain up to date on the case history. "That was before my time in this precinct, but I remember the case. You guys got a fair amount of bad press for letting it go cold. I hope you have better luck this time. Don't make me look bad. Got it, Johnson?" He gave her the "Green Light" to re-open the case and to regroup her team. Three years ago the bastard duped them. He remained one-step ahead of them. What frustrated law enforcement from both states, was the abundance of evidence recovered from the crime scenes. Yet, the "Ghost" as they dubbed him, or her, did not exist in any law enforcement database. Rhonda had a gut feeling that reopening this case would be the "death of her."

As Detective Johnson sat at her desk trying to remember as many details of the case as possible, her desk phone rang; startling her.

"Detective Johnson. Talk to me." "Rhonda, it's Anne Spencer." Rhonda expected a call from the DA's office, just not so quickly. "Have you gotten the 'Ghost' case back yet?" "Hello, ADA Spencer. I'm fine and how are you?" "Sorry, Rhonda. It's just that I received a call from the NY Director of the FBI. It looks like the bastard is back in business." "I know, Anne; as a matter of fact, I literally left Captain Delgado's office ten minutes ago. Earlier, I received a call from Detective Bill Reynolds, from West Hartford. He and I spoke for a while. It was his call that brought me into the loop first. We are assembling the old team and plan to work the case as a joint task force again. I was going to call you later this afternoon. I'll keep you informed as things progress. How are you doing? And, how are those adorable twins?" They spoke a little while about their personal lives and what was happening since they last worked together three months ago. "Listen to me, Miss Anne. I have a friend who's a cop in the 1st precinct. That's your neck of the woods on Long Island, right? He's a really nice guy, and kind of easy on the eyes." She could hear Anne exhale as she sighed. "Andrew's coming home. He always does." "Anne, it's been over a year. Trust me on this; you need to seek out male companionship. Just go to dinner; have meaningful adult conversation with the opposite sex." Rhonda knew her words fell on deaf ears. "Maybe you should follow your own advice, Rhonda." After a moments pause, Anne said, "I'll think about it. Really, I will." "Girl, you said that three months ago, but, alright; when you're ready. And, don't you worry about me, I never follow my own advice. Keep in touch, ADA Spencer." "I promise, Detective." She paused, and then added, "Thanks, Rhonda."

Chapter 22 – We need to talk

Alice sat at her computer staring at a picture of her lake. Apparently, the screen saver had kicked on. To her dismay, she realized that in her absence of mind, the day had all but disappeared. By some miracle, she had somehow written almost fifty pages. The real lake, now reflected dark shadows of the homes and trees as dusk fell upon it. She spent the earlier part of the day with Jeff. Her heart pounded, recollecting the moment they kissed again. They walked along the edge of the lake talking and holding hands. Jeff made a lame but sweet effort to seduce her. She remembered ruining the moment by mentioning Robert. She had no idea why she did such a stupid thing. Besides, she had a good idea that her downstate boyfriend cheated on her.

I should call Jeff.

The phone rang six times; Jeff did not answer. Alice hung up knowing that leaving a message was not an option. Jeff was young. She probably told him she needed to work, and he most likely went to a bar to "hang out." She paused in thought for a moment; then despite her better judgment, dialed Robert's cell phone. He did not answer either. Disappointed or relieved, she wasn't sure, Alice hung up and dialed his number again. Still no answer; this time she decided to leave a message. "Hey, Rob. I'm already downstate, doing some shopping. I'll call you when I get back to my apartment. We need to talk. If a late dinner is OK, that would be great." She left the message, feeling a bit guilty lying about her whereabouts, and for what she planned to say to him in person. She had no idea what prompted her to go to the city, but in hindsight it was a good idea. She needed to get things out in the open. Robert's job, and his supposed new client, required him to travel back and forth to Hartford. They were mostly day trips, but on occasion, he stayed over. She wondered if he had gone there today. Perhaps he was staying the night. Maybe he had company. She cleared her mind and rationalized the end result of all this. Alice really liked the handsome and caring guy at house #12. She needed to pause things with Robert so she could follow her heart and see what might develop with Jeff. If Robert cared enough for her, he would end any affair he was having, and fight for her. Alice pondered the possibility that he might be relieved. Perhaps he was done with her, anyway. Thinking of that possibility, she should have been upset, but instead she smiled. She considered Robert's potential dismissal of their relationship as a good thing.

Alice packed an overnight bag. Her heart raced from her anticipated showdown with her more than likely; soon to be, ex. Alice made her way to her car. The driveway gravel crunched under her feet producing a rhythmic beat. She took a lengthy gaze at her beautiful lake with its shimmering reflections. It looked like a Leonid Afremov painting. She imagined Jeff holding her in his arms, with a beautiful sunset as their backdrop. She got in the car and started the engine. The radio played Pink Floyd's "Wish You Were Here." Images of her and Jeff having sex at the edge of the lake flashed in her brain. It seemed so real; as if it actually happened. Then it happened again as darkness fell upon her. The last thing she envisioned was a momentary flash of a body in the water, and blood on her hands.

We are not going to do this; we need Robert!

Robert's name echoed in her head as she awoke from her horrible daydream. It was dark. She must have been out and unaware for at least thirty minutes. The car was still running. Alice backed out of the driveway, her tires following the only set of tracks embedded in the gravel. There were times when Alice would stand at the edge of her driveway staring at it. To her it represented her loneliness in life. The one set of etched tire tracks. No one ever visited her. She never asked Robert to come upstate. She always made it clear that the lake house was her haven for solitude. A place for her to free her mind and write. She never asked him, but often hoped that

Robert would surprise her with a visit. She used to fantasize him seducing her as the moon glowed outside her bedroom window. Lately, those fantasies dwindled; replaced by the young man who literally seduced her without her even knowing it. Whatever psychological issues she was having, she needed to get a grip. One of these days, one of those episodes could get her killed. She could deal with the voice for now. But, the loss of time and waking up in places she never planned to end up; that she could not deal with. "Call Jeff." The car's hands free app responded, "Dialing Jeff." It rang four times, "Come on, Jeff. Answer and I'll turn this thing around and come to you." After ring number five, Alice ended the call. She hated that he did not have an answering machine.

"Damn it, Jeff!"

Give it up Alice; he's not going to answer you.

"Shut Up, damn it!"

Alice almost hit the center divider as she screamed at herself in an attempt to clear her mind from the random chatter in her head that made her crazy.

Chapter 23 – No DNA

Detective Johnson sat at her desk reviewing piles of unsolved murders. She was looking for the slightest connection with the killers M.O. Her Hartford counterpart would likely be doing the same thing, in preparation for the joint task force meeting. The most up-to-date report indicated the cause of death to be a result of asphyxiation. There were no signs of strangulation using rope or any other material. The coroner noted "probable suffocation by human hand, along with minor bruising to the abdomen and right hip area, indicating blunt force trauma." The file included photographs of the victim. Bruises on her neck and face clearly indicated the use of extreme finger pressure. Rhonda closed her eyes, visualizing the attack in her mind as if she were sitting in movie theater. *This poor girl got slammed while out for a peaceful jog in a beautiful park. She must have felt safe. She should have been. Then this bastard knocks her down and takes her life.* The report also indicated the belief that the killer probably lived in New York or possibly Westchester County and made his way to Connecticut. Hartford was a good distance for a serial killer to travel to from the city. It was an odd assumption. She would think more about that, later.

The coffee area was a mess again. "Damn. Doesn't anyone ever clean up after themselves?" She caught a few of the slothful cops looking her way. Loudly Detective Johnson called out, "What? You all think I'm the cleaning lady? Well, hell no!" She pushed a few donut wrappers aside and poured herself a cup of black coffee.

Quietly to herself she said, "Fools, I hope they get a roach in theirs."

"Johnson! There's a call for you on three." Rhonda quickly made her way to her desk and picked up the phone. "Detective Johnson here." The female voice on the other end identified herself as Officer Bines from the Monticello police department. Jeff Donovan's body had been found floating at the shoreline of the lake. Evidence taken from the crime scene showed no matches to any open cases. However, the MO triggered a hit during a secondary search, indicating a possible link to the serial killer cases. Rhonda Johnson's name appeared on the file as the lead detective. The officer also confirmed to Detective Johnson that they also sent out DNA found on the victim, for analysis. After updating Rhonda and getting a few details from her, Officer Bines put Sergeant O'Malley, one of the Monticello detectives assigned to the case, on the line. He filled Rhonda in with more details and added, "A neighbor saw the victim having sex with a blond woman at the edge of the lake. The next morning, she peeked out her window and saw a phalanx of police on the lake and on shore. She gave little information, telling the officers she was "too embarrassed to look on any further." Another neighbor, taking an early morning walk, spotted the body floating a few feet offshore.

"Any idea who the woman was?" Rhonda sounded hopeful as she asked the obvious question. The detective responded with, "Well, as a matter of fact, yes. We showed pictures of all the homeowners to our bashful eyewitness. Fortunately, the Homeowner's association had holiday pictures and driver's license photos for each registered owner. Our witness picked out one Alice Beekman, whose home is a few down from the victim's." Rhonda asked, "Alice Beekman, the author? No shit." "No shit, Detective. We went to her house; no one was home and no car in the driveway. Our forensic team is certain the car was there until around six or seven last night. Another neighbor from the home next to Miss Beekman said she travels back and forth downstate to the city where she has another residence and supposedly a boyfriend." Rhonda sighed, "So she's a player, two-timing her men?" "Could be, Detective. Could be a love triangle, gone bad." Rhonda asked, "Do we know if she conducted any business or book tours in Connecticut? Maybe Hartford?" The Monticello detective told her that he had no idea and suggested she follow up with the writer's agent, "Whoever he or she is."

Rhonda gathered her team and directed them to start gathering information on Alice Beekman. She told them, "Right now, Miss Beekman is just a person of interest." She added, "Let's keep this quiet until we get more information on her possible involvement." Rhonda scanned the squad room and loudly said, "Someone please find out her address here in the city."

Chapter 24 – Alice at home

Robert still did not answer his cell phone. After three tries, Alice decided to call his office. His assistant told her that Mr. Evans' schedule showed that he was taking a few hours of personal time that morning. She expected him back in the office later in the day. Alice was worried that something might have happened to him. Then, something clicked in her mind, and she suddenly became suspicious. *Oh, my god! He's with her.* Alice had no face to match the woman she imagined having sex with Robert. *No, sister. That would be me and, I'm here with you.* Alice shook her head to get rid of the crazy thoughts running amuck in her mind. She dialed Robert's cell phone once more. He finally answered on the fourth ring. "Hello?" "Oh, my god! Robert, are you OK?" Robert's voice sounded strange. "Alice? Yes. I'm fine. What time is it?" He paused and answered his own question, "Oh, shit. It's after ten. I overslept. I took a sleeping pill last night. Sorry, babe, if I scared you. Where are you?" Alice told him, "I'm home, in Brooklyn. You did scare me." Alice thought it strange that Robert's secretary knew he was going to be late. She wondered if he was lying about last evening's whereabouts. "I called you last night and left a message that I was coming downstate. I wanted to meet you for a late meal. When you didn't answer all night, and then this morning again, I had no idea what to think."

"I'm so sorry, Al. Crap! I had better get to work; I have a busy day. How about dinner tonight?"

Alice hung up, disappointed and confused. Robert did not seem to be very interested in talking with her or concerned about her unplanned visit downstate. She planned on breaking up with him. It would be easier if he admitted to an affair. She started having reservations about what she came to Brooklyn to do, so she decided to call Jeff. Alice hoped that hearing his voice would reaffirm her decision. Her upstate friend became her rock. The sound of his sweet and sincere voice would help her get it together. After all, he wanted to help her, and she knew he could. There was something genuine and safe about him. Yet, he stirred a desire in her that she had never experienced before.

Again, no answer. Alice took a sip of coffee. This is not how she planned for her day to play out. She had no idea how much worse it would be, until she heard the knock on her apartment door that would change everything.

"Would you like a cup of coffee, Detective?" Detective Johnson accepted graciously. "Sorry, I don't have any donuts." Rhonda grinned. "I mean or any cake or anything. Sorry." Alice looked embarrassed. "It's all good Miss Beekman. I get that all the time. People assume it's a cop thing about the donuts and coffee. Truth is; it is. Coffee works. Thank you." Alice smiled and inquired why the detective was at her home. Rhonda asked several questions and avoided answering Alice's for the moment.

"Are you acquainted with a Jeff Donovan?" Alice's stomach churned up acid. She had no idea why, but guilt in addition to angst overcame her. *Be careful what you say, Alice.* "Stop it!" "Excuse me Miss Beekman, what did you say?" Alice pulled herself together, doing her best to block out the noise in her head.

"Of course I know Jeff. He's a friend. What about him?"

"Are you two more than friends? Say, romantically involved?"

"No! Well sort of. But, we're not together."

"I guess that would be because you have a boyfriend here as well?"

"No! Well, sort of. Yes. It's complicated." *Not really.*

"Look, Miss Beekman..."

"Please, Alice. Detective, what is this about?"

"Miss Beekman; Monticello police found Jeff Donovan early this morning; dead. They consider it to be an apparent homicide."

Dizziness along with nausea overcame Alice. For the moment, she was in a state of disbelief and total shock. Like a scene out of a horror film, bloody images of a faceless body floating in water flashed through her mind rapidly and then disappeared. *See, I told you! I told you not to fall for him! No good could come from any of that.* "Oh, my god." Alice said the words faintly. Detective Johnson offered a hand to help steady her. With tears streaming down her cheeks, Alice asked, "How? When did this happen?"

"Well, Miss Beekman, that's why I'm here. The local boys got the *when* part figured out. I'm certain they will come up with the *how* part as soon as the autopsy is completed. The *why*, we may never know. More importantly is, the *'who' in the whodunit*. That's the tricky part of the puzzle." The detective's eyes locked firmly on Alice's, making her even more uneasy. "Perhaps you can help. Where were you Sunday afternoon?" Alice made the strangest face; she appeared stressed. At first, Rhonda viewed her reaction as expected for a friend and lover who just found out about their untimely demise. Alice wiped tears from her face, "I was at my lake house until around dinner time. Earlier, I had a drink with Jeff and then we took a walk by the lake. I'm not sure what happened next; I mean I had work to do, so after our walk, I headed back to my house. Please, detective. Please tell me what happened to him." Then, as if she was lip-syncing, Alice blurted out, "Are *we* a suspect?" She had no idea where those words came from. Rhonda heard Alice refer to herself as "we" but dismissed it as nerves. Ignoring Alice's question, the detective calmly asked, "And where were you after dinner?" Alice again looked confused. "I, I…" She remembered ending up back at her apartment in Brooklyn. She also remembered why she went there and that Robert was MIA. "I drove downstate to my apartment." *Maybe Robert drove upstate to see you; and found him! Keep your mouth shut, or you'll lose him too.* Alice's stomach turned inside out. Nausea, and the need to puke, followed. She ran to the bathroom and closed the door. Rhonda sat for a moment, her detective's intuition aroused. She reached into her pocket and pulled out a plastic baggie that she kept for collecting impromptu evidence. "Come to mama." Alice had left a napkin on the table that she had used to wipe her tears. After returning the baggie to her pocket, Detective Johnson waited another minute. "Are you OK, Miss Beekman?" Sobbing sounds came from behind the bathroom door. "Miss Beekman; Alice, please come out." Alice slowly opened the door. "I'm so sorry. I can't believe this is happening." Deadpanned, Alice asked, "Do I need a lawyer?" Rhonda asked, "Did you do something that would require calling an attorney?" Sarah fought to control the moment; fortunately, to no avail. Alice replied, "No. Of course not."

Alice poured more coffee. Rhonda allowed her to calm down before continuing her questions. "Can you tell me what happened at the lake that afternoon?" Alice described the walk she and Jeff took that day and how kind Jeff had been to her. "We were intimate one time; it happened a week earlier. After walking for a bit along the edge of lake, we headed back to his dock area. We spoke for a few minutes. I told him that I had a boyfriend. I don't remember much else of the conversation except that I had work to do, so I left and walked myself home. A few hours later, I decided to go downstate and tell my boyfriend the truth. I planned to tell him we needed a break." Rhonda shook her head. "And how did Mr. Evans take the boyfriend card you laid on him?" "He was very understanding. We had quickly become very close friends. Nothing changed, except that he wanted more from our relationship. I didn't realize until later that day that I wanted more, as well. That's why I'm here in Brooklyn." Rhonda thought to herself, *how interesting: one minute she does not remember the conversation, the next she remembers how understanding he was*. The detective's questions started to appear to Alice as accusatory; this angered her. She felt an uncomfortable loss of control. *Tell her to fuck off and find the real killer.* "Detective, isn't this is out of your jurisdiction? Why are you here? I'm sure the Monticello police are handling the case." Alice pulled another napkin from the napkin holder in front of her. She wiped her nose and asked, "Please, tell me the name of who is handling the case upstate. I'll go back tomorrow and see them."

Rhonda thanked Alice for her cooperation, and offered her condolences. "Oh; I forgot to ask. How did your boyfriend take the news?" *Uh, Oh. The bitch is good.* "He didn't. Robert wasn't home last night, and I couldn't reach him until just before you knocked on my door." The detective's gaze turned bone chilling. Guilt riddled Alice, even though she hadn't done anything wrong. Rhonda handed Alice her card, "Call me if you think of anything else."

"Oh. There is one more question Alice. Do you ever make your way to the Hartford area? Say for book research?" Alice thought, of saying "No, but my boyfriend goes there for business." She held her tongue realizing anything she said could bring trouble her way.

"No Detective, can't say that I have, not recently. What does that have to do with what happened to Jeff?"

Rhonda grinned, "I suppose it has nothing to do with him, or you. Again, thank you for your time, Alice.

As Detective Johnson started her car, a tap on her driver's side window startled her. She lowered the window half way. Alice stood there; she looked different all of a sudden. She looked confident and calm; Rhonda didn't know what to expect. "Sorry, detective. There is something else. Jeff and I had sex that afternoon, down by the lake. I was too embarrassed to admit it, but I don't care anymore. It happened after I told him about Robert. It was then that I knew I had fallen in love with him." Sarah had to cover for Alice. Hiding that lustful event would have raised suspicions. Alice, in a rare moment of clarity, was conscious of what her other self just told the detective. Alice stayed in the background allowing Sarah control over her words. Like reading from a script, she improvised, keeping within the context of the moment. "When I left Jeff, all was good with us. I hadn't told him I was going back to the city to talk to Robert. I didn't know that myself until after I got home." Rhonda smiled. "So, now what? Will you still tell Robert, all this that you just told me?" "If it's all the same, detective, what's the point? I'll tell him I had a friend upstate who was…" She choked at her attempt to say *murdered*.

Rhonda had a lot to consider. She hoped the local police didn't think she was interfering in their investigation. She pondered if the suspense writer's ominous change of persona told her a story made up of fiction, truth, or a combination of both. Could this Robert guy have found out about his girlfriend's infidelity? Perhaps he sought revenge. Still, she had no real evidence of any kind tying this case to her serial killer. Without any, this upstate investigation was not hers to deal with. She would have to wait for the DNA results. Rhonda sensed there was more to this Alice Beekman. A complexity that will bring more surprises to the case. The big question was; which case?

Chapter 25 – Afternoon Delight

"What are you doing for lunch?" "It depends. Who's asking?" Visually, both sisters were impossible to tell apart. Robert had never seen them together, but surmised that seeing them side by side would not help. Distinguishing between them over the phone was indeed, impossible. Robert needed to be careful. He hoped she would play into his rhetoric. "Who do you want it to be? Do you want sexy and exciting or cute and dull? I can be whoever you want me to be." Before Robert had a chance to respond to what promised to be a question with no right answer, she continued with her tantalizing banter. "In addition, and before you answer; I'm wearing the undergarments you liked so much at last week's party. The ones you meticulously chose for me." Not normally a mind-game player, Robert became anxious. Sarah started using big words like her sister, the writer. There were so many little things; similarities that confused him. He figured it was all part of *their* game. "OK, Sarah. Where? I can only get away for an hour."

"Sarah! You said that name again. Sarah!" She paused for a second. She could tell Robert was considering whether, he had slipped-up. "So, Sarah is the one you really want in you bed, isn't she?" Robert stuttered, "Um, hold on a second." The laughter on the other end of the phone disconcerted him. "You are such a silly man sometimes. My sister is at home sulking. You can deal with her later. I want you badly." Sarah whispered a few things she planned to do to him. Relieved from Sarah's poor taste in humor, Robert said, "I'll meet you at my place in fifteen."

It seemed unnatural that two sisters, even identical twins, looked so much alike. He had known a few twins, even dated one. Just one of a pair. He always managed to find some differentiating thing to distinguish between the two. Then again, his previous twin girlfriend and her sister never played him. At least he was mostly sure of that. However, Sarah and Alice, except for hair and makeup, had two completely opposing personalities. This intrigued Robert. It excited him. If forced to choose, Alice was down to earth and more of a sure thing. She was predictable. He would probably eventually marry Alice. Most importantly, Robert trusted her. On the other hand, Sarah was a player. She enjoyed life, and sex even more. Robert had no idea how long he could carry on this affair. Subconsciously, he hoped it would never end.

Back in his office, after his afternoon delight with Sarah, Robert figured he should call Alice. She sounded upset when they spoke earlier, and he felt guilty. If Alice tried calling him at his office like last time, he would have to lie again. If she asked about last night and this morning, he would again have to lie or avoid answering her. These deep dark secrets plagued him with guilt. Yet, in an odd way, also made him feel powerful and in control. Alice could never cope with the truth. Sarah, in some twisted way, would find it exhilarating. If he told Sarah he was a maniac psycho serial killer, she would find it sexy. Robert dialed Alice's cell phone. After three rings, he hung up, not leaving any message. About fifteen minutes later, Alice called him. "Hey, there. I saw you tried to call me. I worked all morning and must have dozed off. Are we still on for tonight? We need to talk?"

Alice decided to tell Robert everything about the previous week's events; mostly everything. She figured the detective would speak with him eventually, and she wanted to get out in front of the situation. After hanging up with Robert, she decided a shower was in order. It had been a rough day. Alice unbuttoned her blouse before sitting on the bed and removing her tight fitting jeans. The sexy undergarments were not what she remembered putting on that morning. She reserved them for date night with Robert. *If you had your way, Jeff too*. Her mind messed with her so often that she found it easier to simply accept most things that she could not explain. From time to time, more often lately, the annoying voice in her head told her things. Sometimes hurtful; at times helpful. She considered paying closer attention to the messages. Jeff would have advised her to listen closely and interpret the meaning of the subliminal noises. He might have thought she was crazy, but he most assuredly would have twisted it in a positive direction. As she continued to undress, she noticed his scent. Robert was all over her clothes. Again, she allowed herself to believe that her mind played tricks on her senses. Aloud to herself she said, "Maybe I still love him. He'll always be with me."

Too bad you cannot remember; he was awesome in bed.

Chapter 26 – Headlines

The newspaper headline read,

*"**Upstate resident found murdered, body floating in lake**. Sources revealed that this might be the work of a serial killer reemerging after a three-year hiatus. Well-known author, and Brooklyn resident, Alice Beekman, who owns a lake home in Monticello, NY where this horrific crime occurred, is being questioned as a person of interest."*

The article continued to profile Alice and her success as a fiction novelist. The reporter emphasized her long-standing reputation. He was kind enough to ease off focusing solely on the murder, or her possible connection to the victim. She was certain other news reports would soon emerge. She feared they would not be as kind, as they painted her portrait with their words.

Alice's phone rang, waking her up from a much-needed nap. Robert sounded agitated. "Did you see the late edition of the Post?" He read it to her, and told Alice to turn on the TV for the news. "Oh my god, Robert. I planned to tell you tonight when we met for dinner. I only found out about all this, this morning, when a detective came to speak with me." Alice turned on the television. The five o'clock news edition had just started. Robert said nothing as they both watched the same broadcast from their own apartments. The news reporter, not revealing her sources, told the story pretty much the same as the newspaper did earlier in the day. Then came the bombshell of all bombshells.

"This just in; Mary Martin reporting, on location from Monticello, upstate New York." The reporter repeated the same story again, this time showing video of the crime scene and Jeff's house. The camera panned along the shoreline using fancy time-lapse editing, to a view of Alice's lake house. After a minute of the reporter giving a condensed biography of Alice, they switched back to the crime scene. At the edge of the lake, the reporter interviewed an elderly woman. A rolling banner at the bottom of the screen read, *"Local woman witnesses well-known author and victim together shortly before the coroner's estimated time of death. Police say she is the only eyewitness, so far."*

"I didn't see that poor young man being murdered. However, she and he, that poor boy and the writer; they did things; sinful things that made me hide my eyes. I drew my curtains and didn't open them until this morning; all the commotion woke me. I saw the police and rescue workers down here. That's when I heard what happened."

Alice was mortified. Robert remained silent on the other end of the phone. She heard his fast-paced breathing; she sensed his anger. "Robert, this report is all wrong. It was not me. It couldn't be." Robert angrily said, "It couldn't be? It sure sounds like you. Who else would it be? Maybe your twin sister?" He wanted to take it back as soon as he said that last part. He was hurt and jealous. Jealous of a dead man. Mentioning her sister could ruin everything. Evidently, and for whatever reason, she did not want him to know about Sarah. Oddly, Alice seemed to ignore his comment about her sister. It was as if he had not referred to her at all. He calmed down and asked, "Did you do it?" Alice sobbed, "I told you I didn't have sex with him that afternoon. That old woman is either mistaken, or lying." Agitated, Robert asked, "Did you *ever* have sex with that guy? How did you know him?" Alice sobbingly said, "Can we meet and I'll tell you everything?"

"No Alice, tell me now!"

Alice reluctantly explained how she met Jeff. That he was simply an acquaintance, a neighbor. She told him about that one night after she had gotten very drunk. "I had no control over what I did that night. I didn't even remember going to the bar let alone, home with him." She explained how comforting and understanding Jeff was during her meltdown. She added, "The situation just happened." She told Robert that she and Jeff formed a friendship. "He wasn't judgmental, which made it easy to tell him things." She also explained to Robert that she came downstate to tell him everything, but all this exploded before she got the chance. Robert asked, meekly, "Did you fall in love with him?" Alice took a breath before answering. *Tell him no!* "I don't know exactly how I felt; or, how I feel right now. All I know is that I do *love* you, and I wanted to tell you, and talk to you about it. We have always told each other everything, good and bad. I'm sure you would be honest with me if this was all reversed. The timing messed it all up for us. I'm so sorry."

Robert had no idea how to react to this unexpected turn of events. He also felt deep-seated guilt. Guilt over his own infidelity. Alice seemed confident that he would handle the issue with honesty if he were the one who cheated. A few hours earlier, he and Sarah had sex in his apartment, in his bed. Alice and he had spent many nights in that same bed. What the hell was he thinking? He needed to sort things out for himself. "Listen, Alice. Let's not do tonight. We both need a little space; a day or two to try to figure this all out. You should seek legal representation, a good criminal lawyer, in case this thing takes a bad turn in your direction." He realized as he said it that he had questioned her involvement. Alice realized

Rob might not have her back, and that she may very well be on her own.

****

Later that afternoon, Detective Johnson returned to her precinct. She reviewed her notes along with the photos she had taken earlier. Rhonda wasn't sure who was involved or what they were involved with, but something seemed off with this Alice Beekman and the boyfriend, Robert Evans. Earlier in the day, after the interview, she decided to follow Alice to get a better idea of her character. The detective sat in her car eating the second half of a leftover tuna sandwich and drinking cold coffee. The soft Coleman cooler she always brought with her kept food cold for up to 12 hours. She often joked with her colleagues, 'I'd rather have my cooler than a partner. It provides everything I need and there's no small talk involved." She glanced over to the passenger seat where the open bag sat, and she smiled.

A little after noontime, Alice emerged from her apartment. She had replaced her depressing attire of sweatpants and t-shirt that she wore earlier, during the interview. She now had on a cute pencil skirt. Alice's hair looked all done up and sassy. Even her strut, which displayed confidence, seemed completely out of character. Especially for a woman whose love interest had been murdered less than twenty-four hours earlier. The detective took several pictures of Alice leaving the apartment and getting into a taxi. Rhonda followed the Yellow Cab to a residential area of mostly brownstones. She watched as Alice exited the cab, and made her way up to one of the building's entrances. She snapped a few more pictures. And, a few more of neighbors as they entered and exited. Rhonda sat back, her mind searching for ideas on how this lunatic girl tied into the murder upstate, and possibly her cold case as well. Her cell phone rang, startling her. "This is Detective Johnson!" One of her team members had checked the list of residents living at the street address she was surveilling. As he read the names, she stopped him. "Robert Evans? That's the boyfriend. Just as I suspected. I'll get back to you; thanks." The detective sat back and waited. This was no longer the sad young woman seeking console from her boyfriend. This was a happy little twit whose changed demeanor now made her appear more likely good for the crime.

Rhonda looked around, hoping to find a 7-Eleven or Dunkin Donuts Shop for a fresh, hot cup of coffee. Of course, as luck would have it, this area was all residential. She said to herself, "Damn." She checked the time noting it was 1:45PM. As she looked up, there they were. Standing just inside the alcove of the front entrance, the door half open behind them, Alice moved her hands all over the guy. Click-click, a few more photos. This was no woman in mourning for the loss of a lover, or a friend. And this Robert guy; what a chump. Rhonda shook her head in disgust.

Sarah waved to Robert as she got into a cab. Rhonda waited until Alice's cab drove away. She started her car and quickly made a U-turn. Without warning, the cup on her dashboard flew onto the passenger seat spilling the last few sips of cold coffee. "Damn it to hell!" She stopped the car, and with her foot firmly on the brake, opened her glove compartment seeking something to wipe up the mess. Unfortunately, except for a few pieces of paper and car related stuff; there was nothing that she could use. She noticed that the coffee had splattered all over her cooler. "No, not you too." She exhaled with a huff. "We'll clean you up later." As she drove off, from her rearview mirror she caught the boyfriend walking out of his apartment entrance. She figured Robert Evans skipped lunch and dove right into Alice for dessert. He probably needed to get back to his job. For a moment, Rhonda considered following Robert instead, but then reconsidered it as a waste of time. Alice on the other hand, was somewhat of an interesting enigma.

Chapter 27 – Reality

Alice stood in her cramped kitchen, staring at the refrigerator. She wanted something, but could not remember exactly what. In a blink of an eye, she morphed from sweatpants to fancy skirt. The obscure loss of time during the day, becoming a normal event for Alice, she simply dismissed it. She always felt weird afterward, but usually in a good way. Somehow, her body seemed satisfied. She pondered this for a moment until sadness overcame her. She had the same experience after that mysterious night with Jeff. Little by little, Alice hoped she would put this all together and figure out what was happening to her. She looked in the mirror, realizing that she actually liked how she looked. "I look so pretty. Kind of hot!" She smiled at herself.

Hey, girl. That's my line. And, we are. We are the same, you and me.

Sarah wanted a drink. A real drink. She wanted Jack on the rocks but instead, Alice went to the refrigerator and took out an ice-cold bottle of her favorite brew from Mexico. She popped the cap and sat on the couch. She clicked on the TV, and for the first time all day, allowed herself to unwind.

The loud and incessant ringing of her phone woke her abruptly. Alice sat up, almost spilling her drink. The smell of whisky immediately made her nauseous. "What the hell?" She grabbed her cell phone, "Um, hello. Who?"

"This is Sergeant O'Malley of the Monticello Police Department. I'm sorry to bother you, Miss Beekman. I understand that Detective Johnson informed you of Mr. Donovan's untimely demise. We need you to return here for an interview with the detectives that are working the case. How soon would that be possible?" Alice was still groggy from her nap. She had a reasonably good day and finally relaxed for a short time. This phone call undid all of that, and more. Her mind became addled again. *Don't agree right away! Put it off for as long as you can!* Alice ignored the voice in her head. She would have to confront the issue eventually. Besides, there would be a funeral and she wanted to attend. Whatever happened to Jeff, she, in some way, felt she was culpable. She had no idea why. "I'm sorry officer; I mean Sergeant. I have business to take care of tomorrow. I can come in on Thursday, say around 11AM; does that work?"

Sergeant O'Malley hesitated, but then told her he was OK with Thursday morning. He was clear that she needed to be there, and not delay any longer. After she hung up her call with the Sergeant, sadness overcame her once again. Tears again filled her eyes; she already missed

149

Jeff. The kindness and affection he showed her, his understanding and compassion, was something no one else, even those closest to her, ever afforded her. Alice picked up the phone and dialed Jeff's cell phone. She simply needed to hear his voice. The phone rang twice. Alice leaned over and pulled a tissue from the compact box on her nightstand. The third ring silenced, her heart pounded in anticipation. In some mystical way, she expected Jeff to answer the phone. "Hello?" Alice thought, "Oh my God!" *Oh my God, Oh my God.* The echo in her mind was like someone else mocking her. There was silence for a second; neither party on the line said anything. Then he spoke again. It sounded like Jeff. Alice again became lightheaded and considered hanging up. "This is Eric Donovan, Jeff's brother. Who's calling?"

God have mercy, girl. Speak up! Alice said, "Eric?" She sniffled, "I'm so sorry for your loss. This is Alice Beekman, your neighbor from a few houses down on the lake." Eric's voice was curt, "I am well aware of who you are. Jeff told me about his relationship with you. We speak," he paused a second as his voice cracked. Alice could sense his sadness. "Spoke about everything. What do you want, Alice?" Alice sensed the alienation in his voice. "Jeff and I had a special friendship. We became very close. I cared a lot for him and I know he felt the same about me. I'm devastated and confused as to what happened." Alice paused momentarily. She could hear Eric's breathing becoming heaver by the second. I called hoping to hear his voice, I just wanted..." Do you have any more information you can share with me; anything." Alice paused for a moment; the silence was deafening. "I also want to attend the funeral." Eric sniffled; she thought she heard him blow his nose. Then he abruptly said, "Well, Alice. Jeff did tell that me he cared for you; more than you probably realize. He told me you had other relationship commitments. I told him you were going to break his heart. We argued over my opinion. Now I don't even get the opportunity to tell him, 'I told you so!' You took him away from his family. You are not welcome at his funeral. As for what happened. I also understand you are meeting with the police this week. We'll let them figure out what happened." Suddenly Alice realized that she was probably a suspect; at least as far as Jeff's family was concerned. She expected questions from the local police; that would be normal. Detective Johnson's involvement still made no sense to her. Alice sensed a panic attack approaching. *Easy sister, we both know you're innocent. I took care of what needed to be done.* The voice in her head had a life of its own, making it difficult to discern between reality and daydream. This made her feel even more agitated. Alice gritted her teeth so hard, she feared they would grind themselves to dust. Through her teeth she muttered, "Shut the fuck up! Stop it!" On the other end of the line, Eric said, "He said you had issues. He never used the word 'crazy'. In my opinion, he was deluding himself. He definitely understated your mental state. Stay away from me and my family. Own up to what really happened."

Devastated, Alice laid down on her bed and cried. She now understood how it all looked. Witnesses are saying she and Jeff had wild and rough sex in broad daylight. Hours later, someone finds Jeff dead, and Alice is downstate. She would suspect herself. Then again, she did experience another one of her blackouts. She never could account for the lost hours, sometimes days. Maybe she *did* do this. But, why? She cared about Jeff. She was falling in love with him.

Alice dozed off into a deep slumber. She dreamt of walking along the shoreline holding hands with Jeff. He kissed her gently. The touch of his soft lips on hers sent tingles throughout her body. She wanted more, but guilt made her pull back. A darkness moved across the lake. Shadows emerged from the trees. She was now the aggressor, passionately seducing him. He tried to resist. He wanted to slow her down, but there was no stopping her. She was on top, moving up and down on him. He still tried to slow her. Even in the dream, it was as if she was watching from above, looking down on herself and him. Jeff's face showed his concern for what they were doing and where they were doing it. He tried to sit up, but she pressed her hands firmly on his chest. She leaned into him as he again tried to sit up, and kissed him hard. All Alice saw in her dream vision was her slender beautiful hands pushing his shoulders hard in a sexual rage induced attempt to control him. His head slammed into the slate. She watched as blood rapidly flowed from beneath him. Her face appeared shocked but then changed into a chilling grin. Satan had taken over her body!

Alice sprang into a sitting position just in time, as she puked into her cupped hands. She held her breath and ran to the bathroom.

Chapter 28 – Suspicions

Alice cleaned herself up. Her head hurt; a result of her mind racing with divergent thoughts. Self-analyzing herself, she clearly had feelings for Jeff. Robert, however, had always been there for her until now. He seemed distant and suspicious of her; especially after that damaging and most confusing witness's account of her and Jeff at the lake. The news report of that encounter, of which she had no recollection, could not have happened the way the media and probably law enforcement perceived it. She also considered that Jeff's death might have been an accident, and she plainly could not remember that moment in time. Her dream seemed so real. She knew from her previous encounter with Jeff that her loss of memory resulted in a fantasy dream that turned out to be a reality.

Previously, when Alice experienced an emotionally depressing episode, she would always call Robert for support. He would do his best to console her, which usually meant having sex. Unfortunately, his remedy, while satisfying for the moment, may have been more helpful for his needs than for hers. He lacked understanding of her psyche and he never showed enough interest in actually helping her. She needed him now. Alice hated her selfish motive, but he was all she had for the moment.

Her mom lived in another dimension. Since Alice's teens, her mom acted like a caregiver and not a parent. She stopped being accepting of Alice's quirky personality. Alice was sure Linda did not believe that she had no idea how she became pregnant. The reality being that Linda was well aware of the multiple personalities. Her mom's way of dealing at times, was to deny the split. They fought over the idea of an abortion. Linda begged Alice to abort. Alice agreed one day, and the next refused. In the hospital, her mom again tried, insisting on adoption. Again, Alice flip-flopped. At first she snickered coldly, agreeing it was for the best. Later that day, Alice asked to hold her daughter. Only her mom knew of Alice's mental state. Linda made the deal with *both* personalities, Alice and Sarah, to keep the child, but only if custody be granted to her. This way, Linda would have control of when Alice could see her daughter. Linda also kept a watchful eye to make sure it was Alice and not Sarah. Early on, the expectation that Alice would bond with Grace dwindled. Eventually, Linda kept little Grace's exposure to her mom limited. Alice was aware of her biological relationship to Grace, but remained emotionally detached. Sarah, by all accounts, hers and Linda's, was the real mom. The cold-hearted alter personality had no empathy, which resulted in her inability to love. She only cared about her own selfish needs. Early on, Linda hoped Alice would get her issues under control. She believed that if Alice, as Alice, had the affair that got her pregnant, her relationship with Grace would be completely different.

After several minutes of hesitation, Alice dialed the phone. It rang three times. The caller ID on Robert's screen displayed "Alice." Robert hesitated, letting three rings go by before answering.

"Hey, Alice."
"Hey, Robert. After yesterday, I thought you might not take my call."
"Oh; Sorry about yesterday. You are right. We should talk. How are you holding up?"

They spoke for a while, more like colleagues than as friends or lovers. Robert's demeanor made him appear a bit on the cold side. He seemed to lack compassion for her. Robert told her he had business in Hartford again, and would return on Thursday afternoon. "We can talk more then. I'll call you." Alice told him about her call from Sergeant O'Malley of the Monticello Police Department. "Would you consider coming to the lake for the weekend? We really need to spend some time to talk things over." Robert said that sounded like a possible plan. Even though her feelings remained conflicted, she was disappointed in his lack of commitment. Upon ending the call, neither spoke the words, "I love you" as they usually did before saying goodbye.

Alice poured herself a snifter of scotch. As she did so, she realized how odd that was; she hated scotch. Sarah thought for a brief moment about Robert's frequent trips to Connecticut. There might be a client up there, but not one prolific enough to warrant so many overnight visits. Alice held too much faith in Robert. She trusted him unconditionally. Her naivety sickened Sarah. She would have to deal with Robert. He'd better not be playing her, or Alice.

Chapter 29 – On the Road again

Detective Rhonda Johnson decided that one more night of surveillance was in order. After that, the Monticello police could deal with Alice Beekman. She watched as Alice again exited her apartment. The detective waited as her subject made her way down the block and into her car.

Sarah took Bedford Avenue. The poorly timed lights made following Alice difficult. At least once, Rhonda had to run through a red light without any siren or police lights, since she wanted to remain unnoticed. She continued, maintaining several car lengths behind Alice. As they turned onto Atlantic, traffic flowed smoother. The detective had no idea what direction her subject was headed. Alice continued traveling down Atlantic. Detective Johnson stayed about a block behind her. Without signaling, which really pissed Rhonda off, Alice made a quick right turn. "Damn it!" Caught by the red light at Atlantic and Brooklyn Avenue, a busy intersection, Rhonda had to wait until she could jump it. At the next intersection of Kinston Avenue and Atlantic, she turned and drove up the block. Suddenly it dawned on her, "No shit girl, I know where you are headed." Rhonda had followed this path before, to Robert Evans home. The downstate boyfriend. She made a right onto Herkimer Street. About halfway up the block, she spotted Alice who appeared to be sitting and waiting in her car. Rhonda drove a little further down the block before finding a place to pull over and park. She adjusted her rearview mirror and waited. Oddly, from what she could tell, Alice appeared to be surveilling Robert's apartment building. She said to herself, "Now, this is interesting."

Sarah sat patiently in her car. She suddenly became angry, but had no idea why. She had concerns that Robert had already left his apartment, but she noticed his car parked across the street, just behind where she had pulled over. She considered the possibility that he had lied to her. She also had to deal with Robert's anger with Alice, over her situation with Jeff. Sarah would convince him to forgive her sister. It was all part of the master plan to become Alice. Robert had to stay with Alice. In the end, the lucky bastard would have both his girls in one. Sarah would be in control, and Alice would be stuck down deep in the caverns of hell, where she fought to stifle Sarah until now.

Her handbag was a cluttered mess, with so many odd things in it. If the police searched it, they would be most confused. The bag contained far more varieties of makeup and other various accessories than the average female would normally carry. After all, it contained supplies for two. Oddly, Alice never questioned the eclectic mix of items in her possession. "There you are." Sarah pulled out her cell phone, which was in a hidden zippered pouch inside the handbag and punched in a number. "Hello." "Hey handsome. What are you doing?" Robert sounded hesitant as he replied, "Oh, hi Sarah; I'm just heading out. Where are you?" Sarah felt like toying with him to see what lies he might tell. "I'm at a bar in your neck of the woods. Want to meet up and hang out for a while? I have needs requiring your manly services." Rob gave a short laugh, "Sounds inviting, but I have to see a client in Hartford." Sarah was not done yet. "Too bad. I really am frustrated and need relief. Not to worry, stud, after a few more shots, someone here can fill in for you." After a moment of silence Robert said, "You really are a dangerous one, aren't you? I don't like to share. I can be late. Come to my apartment." "Really, Robert? You don't like to share? Do you hand that line to Alice too? Oh, of course not, she would never put you in that position. She's your faithful little dog. You can have your women and eat them too. Is that how it goes? I'll tell you what. Go on your trip. I'll head home and take care of my own needs. I'm sure the mental image of that meets with your needs as well." Silence, then Rob simply said, "You are a force to reckon with, and I am seriously, turned on right now. I promise to call you as soon as I get back. It wouldn't hurt if you offered a little compassion to your sister. She's in a bad way and might be in serious trouble." Sarah felt anger emerging, she could not be sure if it was hers or Alice's. "Seriously, you're telling me that? You know that we are estranged from each other. You surely do not seem overly concerned for her. Why aren't you with her? Supporting her." She could not believe she just came to Alice's defense. *That is weird*. Robert, lacking in empathy, said, "I'll call you when I get back, day after tomorrow." "Sure." Sarah hung up and waited another ten minutes.

Detective Johnson watched in her rearview mirror as Robert Evans made his way a short distance toward where she was parked, and got into his red BMW. He pulled out and headed back to Atlantic with Alice surreptitiously following him. Rhonda mumbled to herself, "Hmm. This is getting more interesting by the minute. What are you two up to?"

Rhonda checked her wristwatch; Traffic on 678 was moderately heavy for that time of day. Rush hour seemed like a ridiculous time to travel, especially across any of the bridges. Following a moving car in surveillance mode is hard enough under normal circumstances. However, following a person of interest who is following someone else in rush hour traffic, now that's a challenge. Things got easier for both cars following their person of interest once they hit I95. It was slow going as usual for that road. Each of them settled in for the next three hours as they waded through heavy traffic conditions.

As the eight o'clock hour chimed, the trio of cars pulled over on a secluded street, Hamlin Drive. Sarah pulled to the curb a few car lengths behind Robert. As she sat there waiting, she started to get anxious and angry. The homes and apartments were all well maintained, with tree-lined streets and beautiful landscaping. This was a well-to-do, private neighborhood. Why would he be here at this hour of the evening, and not at a hotel or meeting his client at a restaurant?

Detective Johnson drove past both Alice's and Robert's cars, and pulled into a driveway two houses down. Robert exited his car and crossed the street to house number 234. As he approached, the door opened. A little white dog with its tail wagging barked as he walked up the short garden lined path to the front door. Sarah and Rhonda each gazed in wonder as an attractive blonde-haired woman put her arms around Robert, and kissed him. Either he was the client, or she was the client's wife. Either way, trouble was unfolding. Sarah became furious, and started pounding the steering wheel. Alice felt disoriented and confused as to her surroundings. She now looked on as Rob held hands with this woman, and accompanied her into the house. Alice's heart ached. The disappointment was one thing. At least now she understood the reason for his lack of support. He had little time for her. Robert cheated on her, and outright lied about it. She thought about her relationship with Jeff. They had become friends after that one time together. Despite what the news media said, she and Jeff, up to that point, had kept their relationship platonic. She wanted more and planned to be honest with Robert. Robert, the bastard cheater! Her mind played out a fantasy of what she imagined they were doing in the house behind closed doors. Sadness overwhelmed her. Suddenly, her sadness waned; replaced by intense anger driven jealousy. She imagined stabbing Robert, making him bleed. Then, pounding his head on the sidewalk in front of his lover's home. She would paint the words "Cheater!" on the street with his blood. Sarah sat back and calmed herself. She considered going back to New York, but decided to wait awhile and see if he stayed overnight. She would call him either way, in a little while.

Rhonda watched in amazement. She half-expected Alice to get out of her car and confront the cheater and his paramour. The detective wondered what was going through Alice's head.

She had no idea.

Chapter 30 – Phantom of Hartford

The killer sits in a quilted leather office chair while staring at a blank computer screen. The television can be heard from behind, where a commercial for a local restaurant airs. As the commercial ends, the announcer informs his viewers, "SERIAL KILLER STRIKES AGAIN. Stay tuned for the news at six." After a busy day in New York and a grueling bout with rush hour traffic, frustration levels had reached their peak. The killer needed to satisfy an intense urge. The urge to kill. It had been too long since the last enraptured dance with death.

Some people consider death the end of life. And, to others, a chance to do it over again. Or, simply the end of one life here on Earth, and the beginning of another in Heaven. The killer never considered a third choice, where one pays the price for abusing free will by losing it, for all eternity.

The chair swiveled around in a reaction to the newscaster now announcing, "This just in." How exciting to listen to the gory details of another murder. How wonderful it felt to be the contributor of such impressive news. If only they knew why. Perhaps someday, the killer would tell them. While hearing about it sent goose bumps throughout, writing about it was even better. However, the ultimate, was *living* the experience.

The power of taking a life can be exhilarating and euphoric. Not when committed out of necessity, such as a law enforcement officer defending a citizen, or in a war where it's us against them. No; but randomly picking out a breathing subject and squeezing the life out of them ever so slowly. The eyes are the most important to watch closely. Just before the end, the eyes open so wide and the pupils dilate almost as much. The victim's face expresses so much fear; fear out of confusion. Their expressions say what their mouths cannot speak. "Why me? Why are you doing this, to me?"

Oh, the power of taking one's soul.

Strangely, and this happens with some regularity, the murderer loses touch with reality. The television no longer has any news broadcasting. In fact, there is no television. The streets of the upper middle class neighborhood are quiet. Nerves are on edge and the mind has become cluttered with visions of earlier victims. Revisiting what happened in the past is all that can be accomplished while waiting for the next target. A special victim the killer carefully chose. Several nights prior, the killer carefully canvassed the area. People were scoped-out and patterns established.

A dog barks somewhere in the night. The canine's natural attempt to forewarn of its presence, echoes, adding to an already intimidating background. A light mist has just begun to fall. The scene seems so familiar; perhaps a replay from another time? A smile appears on the face hidden in the shadows as the unsuspecting victim approaches. He is still a distance away. He appears to be in his twenties, a nice looking young man. He is the chosen one. Like the jogger running in the park, each had a routine. The killer carefully chose this creature of habit. This sorry soul must have a night job from which he leaves home for after an early dinner. Soon the young man will acquire a once in a lifetime experience. He will become intimately acquainted with death. He will know it's coming, and in the end he will accept it. He will give up and let death take him, for he has no choice.

The streets are deserted. The dog has since quieted down; perhaps he is now safely inside his owner's home. The young man stops at a car, his car, and dangles keys as the alarm chirps, signaling that access to the automobile has been granted.

The killer startles him. "I'm so sorry. I called a taxi over an hour ago. My car down the street would not start and I got impatient, so I started walking. Any chance you are heading into town?" She smiles innocently. "I called my girlfriend, and she's meeting me at the diner on 5th."

Her beauty mesmerizes the young man. He fantasizes about how she can express her gratitude for rescuing her. "Of course. No problem." He reaches out his hand, "Scott." "Nice to meet you, Scott." Her hand is soft, yet unusually strong. In an act of chivalry, the young man walks around to the passenger side and opens the door for his guest. Scott starts the car and glances over at his passenger. She smiles. "You can join my friend and me for a drink, if you'd like. It's the least I can do to repay you for your kindness." He's about to pull out when he notices her slipping off her shoe. Her foot stretches out and brushes his leg. She grins, and it is very sexy. The young man is confused and not sure what his next move should be. He considers that maybe she's a prostitute trying to hook him. The young woman is aware of his shallowness; she had counted on it when she chose him. Her actions turn him on even more, as he reconsiders that she is simply into him and tonight is his lucky night. He puts the car back in park, and turns toward her. She is holding her cute little shoe in her hand. She provocatively licks her already glossed lips. The look on her face says, "I want you, now." Suddenly the shoe pops out of her hand; she makes a cute little squeak of embarrassment and blurts out, "Sorry." He smiles and reaches down to retrieve it. His other hand finds its way to her ankle for support as he reaches under his seat. The circumstances lent itself to him being bold. As he sat back up, he allowed his hand to glide up her leg; she moaned. Tonight was going to be his lucky night. She thought, "This is great fiction."

He thought her embrace would be erotic. At first it was. She kissed his neck and bit his earlobe. Her hand moved methodically across his chest and then down further. Her fingers played down there for a very brief moment before taking a firm grip. He fought off his need to let loose. With her other hand, she brushed his lips teasingly. He closed his eyes and leaned in for a kiss. Suddenly, and without warning, he felt her hands gripping his throat. He had read about Erotic Asphyxiation and believed that's what he was about to experience. Fighting to delay his climax, he realized too late that he was at deaths door.

She looked into his panicked eyes; they were beautiful as they opened wide and then slowly closed. She kissed his forehead in appreciation for *her* relief. Now she could return to her home, fully satiated, and ready to write again.

Chapter 31 – Angry

Detective Johnson followed as Alice abruptly pulled out of her parking spot and sped away. She wondered what Alice would do now. With one of her lovers dead, murdered; and the other, a cheater, Rhonda felt sorry for her. She still had nothing incriminating on Alice relating to the serial killer. As they drove through town heading toward the thruway, Rhonda lost sight of Alice. She assumed the girl would head home, and figured it did not really matter at this moment. The trip across the bridges was a complete waste of time. In Rhonda's line of work, she dealt with all kinds of family disputes. Most involved one or the other partner in an extra-marital, or significant other affair.

The car swerved as Alice wiped tears from her eyes. Her heart had been broken twice in less than one week. Her budding affection for Jeff crushed, she automatically turned to the person she always could count on, until that moment when his lips met another's. He outright lied to her face. Anger overwhelmed Alice as Sarah took control of her beautiful body. She pounded the steering wheel with her fist causing the car to swerve again. "Motherfucker! We'll get even with you." *Maybe there is an explanation.* "Damn you, Alice! You are so submissive that it makes it so easy to screw you over." Her hands clenched the steering wheel firmly making them appear as fists ready to punch the cheater's lights out. *We need to calm down*. Sarah relaxed her hands a bit at the subliminal diversion. Alice had never said we. She had never been a part of anything Sarah did, while dominating consciousness. For the first time, Sarah was unnerved.

Alice continued driving. The traffic had eased up, allowing her to maintain a steady sixty miles per hour. She removed her left hand from the steering wheel, seeking an explanation for the pain she felt. Her palm revealed a deep purple color. Doing the same with the right hand showed the same results. Perplexed, but not shocked, she assumed she had gripped the wheel too tightly in her moment of rage, and then shrugged it off. She turned the radio on. Alice started humming along with the music.

Detective Johnson, tired and disappointed, decided to stop at her precinct before heading home. She exited off the Deegan Expressway onto the F.D.R. Drive. It was after 11PM when she arrived. Most of the detectives went home already, or were at a local bar pounding down a few with their partners. "Johnson!" Rhonda stopped and stared through her tired eyes at the desk sergeant. "Yes, Sarge." "Don't look so pleased to see me." He frowned, which was normal for him and then continued. "You had a call from that West Hartford detective. What's his name?" Rhonda perked up, "Bill Reynolds?" "Yeah. That's the guy." The sergeant extended his hand with a sheet of notepaper. "He left his number and said you should call any time of day or night; but as soon as you get the message." Rhonda snatched the paper, "Thanks."

Chapter 32 – Whodunit?

The squad room, usually running amuck with detectives, thankfully was quiet. With cold, probably half-day old coffee in hand, Rhonda dialed Bill Reynolds' number, squinting as she tried to read the Sergeant's handwriting. She glanced at the clock on the far wall, that showed 11:18PM. She mumbled to herself, "Poor bastard; must be important."

After the fourth ring, Reynolds' voicemail picked up, asking the caller to leave a message. Rhonda left him a message to call her up to 11:45PM. After that, it would have to wait until the morning. "I'll be at my desk by 9AM, call me. Thanks, Bill."

Rhonda took another bitter sip of her almost rancid beverage. "Yuck." At 11:40PM, she grabbed her jacket and tossed the empty coffee stained styrofoam cup into the trash basket next to her desk.

Brrring, Brrring.

"Damn."

"Hello, Johnson here." "Hey, Rhonda. Late night at the office? Puts a damper on relationship management." Rhonda pondered what her colleague just said, "Hey, Bill.

Don't I know it!" Feeling a little guilty for his remark, he followed with, "Sorry, I meant, for finding a new one." Rhonda sighed, "Either way, Bill. It wasn't good for my marriage, and it certainly doesn't make it easy to meet new people. What do you know about that, anyway? You have Doris; she's your golden gal." "I am blessed. Thirty-three years young and we're still on our honeymoon." Rhonda gave a snort as she laughed, "So, what's the trick?" Bill laughed along with her, "We both have jobs with erratic hours that require a good deal of our attention. There's no time for fighting when we're together. We learned to optimize our time." "God bless both of you, Bill Reynolds. I'll try to hold back on my envy." Bill cleared his throat, "Mr. Perfect is out there; when the time is right, it will happen." "I suppose. So why the call at this ungodly hour?" Detective Reynolds cleared his throat again, "I'm afraid I have more news on our case. Not very good news. We had another attack. This time in a residential area during prime-time." The Hartford detective continued on to describe the crime scene, time of the attack, and what evidence they found. Rhonda's heart pounded as she realized she was in that same neighborhood less than two hours earlier. Suddenly, it occurred to her that both her persons of interest were there as well. She lost sight of Alice once they got to the thruway. Maybe Alice doubled back. Bill asked, "So what do you think? What's our next move?" Rhonda,

173

preoccupied in thought, did not respond right away. "Rhonda? Detective Johnson!" "Sorry, Bill." "No problem Rhonda. I don't know what you have going on today but you might consider coming to West Hartford to view the crime scene for yourself." The earlier events and the timing of Bill Reynolds' call changed things. Now, Alice was more than a person of interest. In the last few minutes, she became a suspect. The one oddity is that none of the DNA from previous crime scenes were a match to Alice Beekman. Bill continued, "I'm still going with our serial killer responding to some sort of upsetting stimulus; say, the death of a loved one, or more so, a betrayal of some kind. The unsub goes over the edge and needs a way to relieve his frustration." Rhonda mumbled, "Or her." Bill repeated, "Or her." Detective Johnson was not ready to disclose her earlier field trip. It all seemed to make sense though. Jeff was outside the target areas where she previously acted out her killing spree. Something went wrong that triggered her to take out her aggression on the one person she seemed to truly trust and care for. Rhonda needed to find out what that trigger was. Then, perhaps she would be able to tie things together. As for the cheater, she figured he had better watch his ass. If Alice turned out to be her serial killer, after tonight, he could be next. "OK, Bill. I'll call you tomorrow to discuss the crime scene details. As far as a plan to visit the crime scene, I'll have to get back to you on that. Sorry if I seem distracted. I suppose I'm tired." Bill said good night, and they both clicked off the call. Rhonda headed home for a steamy hot tub session, and then a cozy bed. As exhausted as she was, her mind was moving in hyper-mode. She prayed that sleep would come easy.

Chapter 33 – Sisters

Putting pen to paper always came easy to her. Ever since she was a little girl, she displayed an incredible imagination. At her third grade open-school night, her teacher, Mrs. Klein, told her mom about her wonderful imagination. "Oh, but she also has such a good sense of family. She and I talk often. Some days I forget that I'm talking to an eight-year-old. Anyway, she tells me what a wonderful mom you are and how you take care of her and her little sister. It must be difficult raising them on your own." The little girl's mom suddenly turned pale, as if she had just seen a ghost. "It's only my daughter and me." The teacher looked confused. Embarrassed, she said, "I'm so sorry, I..." "It's OK. There was a twin, but I lost her during childbirth. Her father; we never married. He never acknowledged his daughter. I have consulted with her pediatrician and we had a few sessions with a child psychologist; several, actually. They all assured me she would grow out of her imaginary sister." The teacher had no idea how to react but she compassionately said, "Well, her teachers and I will make an extra effort to help her to be comfortable. Imaginary siblings are common at her age. She will grow out of it soon enough. And, if you're OK with it, I want to keep speaking with her." The mom smiled and said, "Sure. Thank you." As the mom started walking away, she turned back to the teacher, "It's amazing; how they know." She acknowledged the teacher's bewildered look before continuing; "She never met her sister, at least not outside of the womb. I never discussed the loss. I wanted to wait until she was older and able to understand better. That was also the advice of her doctors. Somehow, though, she knows about her." The teacher smiled; the mom turned away and headed out of the school.

Alice lay in a fetal position on her bed back in her Brooklyn apartment. With a box of tissues next to her, and several used ones crumbled all around, she cried. Outside, cars or 5th Avenue honked their horns at pedestrians crossing against the light. Every so often, she heard drivers yelling at the unmindful people as they Jay walked or texted in the middle of the street. She imagined people flipping fingers. The rhythm of the outside sounds soothed her, allowing her to drift into a deep slumber riddled with intense dreams.

The lake had a calming effect. It always helped Alice, when she felt agitated, to walk along the shoreline as she was doing now. Sometimes she would take a walk simply to clear her mind. This enabled her to go back to her house and create works that entertained others. Looking up, the blue sky alternated with fast moving, puffy clouds.

As she stared, the white cotton balls took on various shapes resembling animals and occasionally, people.

"You're my best friend. I could not survive without you." *Her sister's hand had a warmth to it as she held it. They walked along the edge of the lake. They sat down on a flat rock and looked out upon the lake. The water rippled gently as a boat slowly moved along further out. Alice said, "This is nice; me and you like this."* *Her sister asked another question, "Do you love him?"* *Alice answered, "Yes. I think I do. And, I'm sure he loves me back."* *Her sister squeezed firmly before letting go of Alice's hand. "I'm referring to Robert! Not Jeff. We both know he's dead."* Alice, for the first time, looked at her sister. Her heart skipped a beat. She was looking at herself grinning as if in a mirror. Only she was certain there was no grin on her own face. *"I once thought we could both love him, Robert that is. The truth is; he will become suspicious if we both continue to share him."* *Alice asked, complacently. "And, what does that mean?"* *"It means, dear sister, that only one of us can have him. If we were two instead of one, you could have had that Jeff guy. You two were a perfect match; but seriously, he's dead and we cannot change who we are and how we are joined together. Robert wants me. You are lackluster unless you are writing something as fiction. Even then, most of what you write is mine. I own that as well."* *Alice took Sarah's hand, "Look*

at me, I'm Alice. This is my life!" "No Alice, it was your life. Now it's mine and you need to step aside and let me remain in control. It's the only way to keep Robert. It's the only way to keep us safe from that detective and the others who want to do away with us."

Alice woke up abruptly. She felt a pain in her chest. At first, she thought a heart attack, then she realized as it quickly subsided that it was indigestion. The dream seemed so real. She needed Jeff. He understood her eccentricities. This Sarah from her dream, must be her conscience. Maybe she did hurt Jeff. It must have been an accident. "Damn it! Why can't I ever remember things that happen to me?" Alice pounded her fist hard into the bed. She considered speaking to someone like when she was a little girl, a doctor or other professional. Her mom perhaps? But, her mom never truly understood what she was going through.

Those doctors are quacks, go ahead and waste your time. See if I care. Besides, if you mess it up, I'll have to fix it.

Chapter 34 – Truth

Detective Johnson arrived early to meet with her captain about the three-year-old cold case. She explained to him that in light of the new developments from last evening's discussion with Bill Reynolds, and her suspicions that Alice may be involved, she wanted to maintain surveillance. Her boss reluctantly agreed. As Rhonda started to leave his office, he reminded her of the heat they took three years prior for failing to solve the case.

Rhonda sat at her desk, sipping a hot cup of coffee. She had her team researching everything about everyone involved. "You guys get busy. I am going to head upstate. Dixon, you stay on the girl." Rhonda handed a piece of paper with the address and Alice's picture to her rooky detective.

Alice woke up early, showered, and got dressed before heading into the kitchen. She made herself a cup of hot coffee and sat down to read the local paper. On page three was another article about Jeff's "Brutal" murder. *Why torture yourself? This publication is garbage. We write better fiction.* Alice closed the newspaper and pushed it aside. She was well aware that going upstate would be a difficult chore. Between the police wanting to question her and knowing Jeff's family hated her, she wanted to hide in a closet and never come out. Alice felt her weakness wane. Sarah locked the apartment door and headed outside to her car.

The thruway moved slowly in the midst of rush-hour traffic. Rhonda's cell phone rang, "Detective Johnson." "Detective; Dixon here. The suspect is on the move. She just entered the northbound New York State Thruway. How should I proceed?" Rhonda considered the choices before answering. She told her detective to back off. "I've got this, Dixon. You can go back and join the rest of the team. I have a pretty good idea where she's headed."

Two hours and forty-five minutes later, Sarah walked into Montcello police headquarters. She wiped her tough, smart expression from her face, replacing it with Alice's shy, sulking expression. "Sergeant O'Malley, please; I'm here for an interview at his request." The desk Sergeant motioned for Alice to take a seat on the bench across the small vestibule. Sarah looked at it and decided leaning against the wall was a safer, cleaner option. For a moment, Sarah became confused. Alice was fighting for control. Her head spun from the loss of time and location. Par for the course these days, ending up in unplanned places did not faze her. She knew she was certifiably nuts, and she accepted it. *OK, sister. You are better at playing*

Miss Innocent, anyway. The voice she imagined in her head usually made sense to her; as if her mind self-reasoned with itself. At times, she considered she might be clairvoyant. Things happened to her that she had no prior realization of until after the occurrence. Sometimes it took someone else to enlighten her as to what happened. Other times it came to her in a dream that later, in an awakened state, proved itself out.

On the other side of the interview area a sign read, "Central Booking." Detective Johnson looked around the room. She wanted to avoid running into Alice Beekman. "Excuse me, Sergeant; I'm looking for Sergeant O'Malley." Rhonda held up her ID. The desk Sergeant grinned, "He's in, working an interview. You want I should interrupt him?" Rhonda ignored the poor guy's grammar and said, "Alice Beekman?" He nodded and went back to shuffling papers and sipping his cold coffee.

"I'll be honest with you, Miss Beekman; you don't appear to fit the profile for the crime." As he said it, he realized his remark sounded accusatory and possibly sexist. "But, the events of last Sunday as we are aware of them, and the witness who Id'd you, surely raise many questions, making you a person of interest. I'm sure you understand how all this looks; to us." You need to try to remember more details of that day." What he meant was that she needed a more solid alibi. Alice started to become unhinged, depression overwhelmed her, and she began to cry. "I loved Jeff, I would never hurt him!" *But, we did.* Sarah wiped Alice's sincere tears from her face using a tissue the detective had given her earlier. "Am I under arrest?" Sarah tried to say it meekly, without any disdain. "No, Miss Beekman. Not at this time. Please do not leave town until we have more information. I'll be in touch as soon as I know more or have additional questions." His words sounded so clichéd. "You know where to find me, Sergeant, if you have any more questions. I'll cooperate in any way I can to help find the bastard who did this to Jeff."

Rhonda waited for Alice to leave before repeating her request to the desk Sergeant to see Sergeant O'Malley. She and the sergeant spoke for a while. O'Malley gave his opinion on the case telling his New York City counterpart, "Alice Beekman is the only possible suspect so far. Oddly though, she seems so innocent, and her reputation around town indicates nothing suspicious." He added, "However, her convenient lapse of memory during the time of the murder makes me question her involvement in this crime." The Sergeant had no idea of how twisted Alice's mind really was. Johnson and O'Malley spoke a little longer, going over the details of Jeff's *apparent* murder. Rhonda told the Sergeant that she would return home later in the evening. "I'd like to check out the crime scene if that's alright?" Her upstate associate grinned, "Professional courtesy. Of course."

Chapter 35 – The Other Woman

Robert stopped his slow-paced walk for a moment to reestablish his whereabouts. He realized that he had been wandering the aisles of his corner grocery store aimlessly. His mind, laden with guilt, finally caused him to rethink his position in life. The affairs, at first, allowed him a sense of superiority. His relationship with Alice was rock solid. A "twelve" in his book for looks, and a calm, level headed personality. *What more could a guy want?* He asked himself this question more than a few times during the past couple of months. For most guys, that would be it. But, his beautiful and creative woman tended to put her creativity first. Robert understood; writing was her work, her livelihood. Alice had to deal with a lot of pressure from her agent and the publisher. She needed to avoid distractions, hence the house upstate. Projects tended to take about fifteen months to complete. During that time, Alice's relationships had to accept a seventy-thirty split of time. Robert thought he was OK with that. He put more time into his work convincing himself that doing so was a positive outcome of their relationship. Alice often remarked, using the old cliché "Absence makes the heart grow fonder." During those times when Robert felt lonely, he would repeat her words and go about his day. Then Sarah enters the picture. At first he thinks it's Alice done up all sassy in an effort to surprise him; changing up the *girlfriend* experience. He is immediately turned on by her new look and interestingly vivacious personality. They have crazy sex, during which time she tells Robert she is Alice's twin sister. Sarah explains that she and Alice are estranged. However, she does not go into detail. Adding to his grand abuse of power, she tells him she is OK with his relationship with Alice as long as he keeps this affair from her. *What more could a guy ask for*?

As in almost all similar situations, there is usually one additional element that adds complexity. Take his Hartford client, for example. A two-time "Best Business Women" award winner asked him to come to Hartford to discuss increasing her business with his company. Normally, a phone conference or remote video call would be sufficient to deal with such a matter. When it came down to signing contracts, a lunch or dinner meeting would be appropriate. After two years of working with her company, Robert Evans, newly appointed V.P. of Operations, was the only one she wanted to manage her account. After his promotion a few weeks earlier, Rob had to hand off some smaller accounts to other sales reps. He kept a few larger accounts, like Cramer Industries, where his rapport with the client had become the glue holding the relationship together. Madeline Klein fell into that category. When the woman of the year requests your presence, you attend.

Early on in their business relationship, Madeline proved to be a tough customer. She knew coming into a meeting, what the outcome would be. It was "Her way or the highway." Robert found her to be interesting and very attractive in a different sort of way. She had a charisma so persuasive; it was like an electro magnet. Once she drew you in, her force held you tight. Over time, their comfort level increased and she et her guard down. Two months ago, while in NY for a meeting with his group, Madeline made several flirtatious remarks directed toward Robert. After the meeting endec, Robert walked his client to the elevators and thanked her again for a rewarding discussion. He extended his hand, "Madeline; always a pleasure." The look she gave him, unnerved him. Only a few seconds had passed, but her silence added to his uneasiness. As the elevator doors opened, she observed the empty cab and turned to him, saying in a monotone voice, "Why don't you ride down with me?" , she said, "Would you like to complete the contract signing in Hartford?" She smiled cunningly, "Say, Tuesday next week?" Robert responded, "That sounds like a plan." He offered his hand again; she took it firmly and drew him close, whispering in his ear, "Consider staying overnight, we have much to discuss." She pecked his ear gently and let go of his hand. Madeline Klein, woman of the year, looked back over her shoulder, smiling. Her pet's face appeared expressionless as he stood in the elevator. He considered his client, one of the most confident women he ever met. The doors closed; their affair set in motion.

Chapter 36 – Confrontation

By the time Alice had returned to her upstate sanctuary, the afternoon sun had all but disappeared behind the trees lining the far side of the lake. The moment she got out of her car, she had an uncomfortable sense that things were out of sorts. She observed several tire tracks embedded in her gravel driveway that did not belong to her car. A discarded paper coffee cup lay off to the edge nearer to the front entrance. A chill came over her. She considered the possibility that the police and news reporters came by, looking to speak with her. The police did not have a warrant or they would have said something during her interview. They were probably just snooping around outside, found nothing of interest, and left. Impulse made her walk to the rear of the extended driveway that ran along the entire length of the house. Standing on the edge of the recently rebuilt railroad ties that framed the back area of the house, she looked down the hill. The lake seemed calm and a bit sad. Alice understood that her emotions were playing havoc with her mind. All looked normal as she panned the rim of the lake. The chill she felt earlier now morphed into sadness. She was about to turn around and head into the house when something odd caught her eye. Alice shaded her eyes with her hand to block the glare relecting off the water, and refocused on the obscure object situated a few feet from the rim of the lake, near her dock. A sign made out of something similar to a piece of driftwood had been stuck in the rocky edge. The way its creator angled it, allowed her to see the horrific message handwritten on it. Albeit, not as readable for her, as it was to boaters on the water. She imagined neighbors taking a stroll along the shore and pointing to her home. The sign read "Murderer!" with an arrow pointing up toward the house; her house. Alice screeched. "Oh; oh my god!" She wiped tears from her eyes as she made her way to the wooden staircase and hurried down to the lake. She yanked the sign out of the rocks, ignoring a boatload of teenagers yelling something inaudible at her from a distance out on the lake.

Her house seemed unscathed by the traumatic events of the past week. There was no evidence of damage to the outside, or any indication that trespassers went any further than her shoreline. Inside, an empty goblet stained with wine sat on the kitchen counter. Alice opened the refrigerator and as she hoped, found the rest of the wine. She poured it into the already stained glass without rinsing it. The wine was bitter, but she didn't care. Her heart ached. She took one more sip and headed to her bedroom to change.

The afternoon service was set for 3PM. The local paper had all the information posted in the obituary section. Alice thought it was an odd time for a funeral service. Suddenly, she realized that perhaps Jeff's head injuries as well as the decaying effects of the water might have prevented his family from having an open casket viewing. She felt a little queasy as she mumbled to herself, "Jesus, maybe his family decided to have him cremated." Alice realized if that were the case, the police surely would not have released Jeff's body until the investigation concluded.

Alice stood in the back of the chapel trying not to draw any attention to herself. She panned the room and then focused toward the front of the chapel where Jeff's immediate family sat. Alice breathed a sigh of relief at seeing the beautiful mahogany casket situated a short distance in front of where Jeff's family sat. As she imagined earlier, the coffin remained closed. The ceremony was short and only Jeff's brother spoke, giving a heartfelt eulogy. Eric talked about when they were young boys hanging out together and how he looked after Jeff. He told of their strong bond as brothers, and as friends. Eric's eulogy sounded more like a sermon. He expressed his sadness, saying, "Jeff had his whole life in front of him. God will judge those responsible and see that penance is paid for taking him so early." He spoke of the love Jeff bestowed on all of his family, and how much they would miss him. Alice wanted to stand up there and say something nice about the wonderful and caring person Jeff was. She wanted to tell them she was in love with him and that she would never hurt him.

But you did! Hurt him. We should not be here; this is a bad idea.

Alice turned and walked down the four stone steps, hoping to make it to her car unnoticed.

"What are you doing here? You have no right!" Alice turned to find herself face to face with Eric Donovan. With her head down to avoid making eye contact, Alice said, "I'm sorry, so sorry for your loss." She turned away, again trying to escape what would likely be a dreadful confrontation. As she slowly walked away, she said to the silence behind her, "I loved him. I could not have hurt him. Not ever." From behind her she heard Jeff's brother sobbingly say, "You're the writer; tell your fiction to the police. They'll expose the truth about your sins."

We should beat him until his eyes bulge and all life from within is drawn out of his body.

Alice disregarded the voice in her head as she quickened her pace in an effort to escape any further humiliation.

Detective Johnson who had been standing off to the other side of the small group of family and friends, watched as Alice Beekman and Eric Donovan briefly had words. The detective noted that the deceased's family did not welcome Alice at the service. They appeared extremely upset by her presence. Rhonda considered the possibility that this form of rejection could be a trigger to set off the urge for another killing. She wondered, if Alice were the killer, would she need to find another victim? Is the respected author really the cold-blooded serial killer that law enforcement agencies from two states were hunting?

Detective Johnson waited for Alice to pull out of the small parking lot, and disappear down the road. She planned to head home straight from the cemetery, but then considered staying and sitting on the Beekman lake house through the night. She mumbled to herself, "Ok Beekman, the only way to get me off your back is to be at home sleeping when and if another serial killing happens." As she opened her car door, she saw Sergeant O'Malley. He waved his hand signaling for her to wait a moment. She pushed the car door closed and walked towards O'Malley and his colleagues.

Chapter 37 – Janice

"Janice; you are so freaking, funny. You're the only person I know that can joke about her soon to be ex-husband." The small group of friends raised their glasses and in unison, said "Cheers." The thirty-year-old middle school teacher took a sip of her wine. "Screw the bastard, he had it damn good and knew it. His little twerp, twenty something, can have him. I hope she checked the receipt that said 'No Returns,' cause that policy is firm!"

"Here! Here!"

She and her friends all laughed as they poured more wine and enjoyed an eclectic assortment of dinner dishes. "Oh! And, thank you Emily for being an incredible hostess. And, you too, Jake." They all raised their glasses again. Jake poured more wine.

"This evening was most enjoyable. Thank you all for so much love and support. Just one thing." Her friends looked on, waiting for the punch line. She continued, "Who's getting divorced next? I want another party." Her friends laughed as each gave Janice a warm hug. "Really; you guys are the best. I love you all. Thank you. And, with that, I must bid you all, farewell." She made a dramatic curtsey; then stopped for a moment, sitting on the little bench next to the door. After a moment, she stood up again and turned toward the door. A bit off balance, she nearly stumbled. With her cell phone in hand she said, "There we go. Uber is all set."

Janice used the wall to steady herself as she made her way through the looby and out to the street. Once outside, the cool air made her feel more alert. "OK now. Where are you, Mr. Uber?" After a few minutes, Janice became concerned that the driver was not going to show up. She checked her phone and realized that she had entered the wrong address for the pickup. Her friend's apartment was 19 Elmsford. She told Uber 9 Elmsford. "Damn it. I've got papers to mark." She laughed to herself, thinking, "Sure. That might not happen." First Janice walked to the left and checked addresses. They were going up into the 20's. She headed the other direction looking for #9, or her taxi ride.

The fresh air helped clear her head from the effects of the wine she had consumed. The street appeared quiet, even for a mid-week night. She glanced at her watch, noting that it was already 10:20PM. She considered returning to 19 Elmsford to seek a ride from one of her friends, rather than reorder another Uber. The sudden pain was both immediate and excruciating. It seemed to come out of thin air. The school teacher could not have known that she had been struck a devastating blow to the back of her skull by a lead-weighted blackjack. She was unconscious before she collapsed in a heap onto the sidewalk. In an almost nightmarish hallucination, her sense of reality gone, she was helpless, as her assailant dragged her body from the lighted street, into the darkness of a nearby alley. As she slowly regained her senses, all she could see were shadows followed by stars. She realized too late that her ability to take a breath was rapidly diminishing. Panic ensued; Janice flew into a wild rage, flailing to free herself from whatever held her by her throat. She could feel her windpipe being crushed. One hand caught the side of what she thought to be an ear. She dug her nails deep into firm skin tissue. The warm sticky fluid dripping from her assailant's face coated her fingertips. Her attacker barely made a sound; all she heard was her own throaty gasps for air as the surrounding darkness lead her into oblivion.

This was the first time the killer had to deal with a resisting victim. Usually, she caught her victims off guard and subdued them easily. This one reeked of booze, which would account for the bold behavior. The killer knew she had made a poor choice. Her face hurt badly. The discomfort, accentuated by the oozing sticky fluid running down her face was overwhelming; another sensation she rarely experienced. She had selected her target area carefully, placing priority on the lack of adequate street lighting and low pedestrian traffic. With her sleeve pressed to her face wound with mild pressure, she made her way back to the car she left parked a few blocks south of the attack.

Writing things down as soon as possible after they occurred made for better, more precise writing. When she arrived home, she would put pen to paper, or in this case, computer. She considered adding a twist to her story by including the valiant attempt for survival that her helpless victim made. She would leave out her own injuries from the story. In the car, before starting the engine, the killer sat back for a moment and closed her eyes. She replayed the last moments as the woman's eyes opened wide. She could see the terror in them. The killer imagined her soul as it floated upward to nowhere. Serenity replaced rage; the beast was calmed and ready to go home to be creative again.

*****

Patty and Mike held hands as they crossed 5th Avenue, and made their way on to Elmsford. The teenagers spent the night playing "beer pong" at a friend's house. Mike put his arm around his girlfriend and said, "Wow, this street is really dark; hold on to me." Patty wrapped her arm around Mike's waist as he held her tighter. Excitement ran through her body. Happiness took on a new meaning for her. Mike was her first boyfriend. Right now, in her mind, he would be the only one. She said, "It's dark, and kind of creepy." To herself she thought, "Good excuse, Mikey; hold me close and don't let go." Patty leaned into Mike and kissed him. They both fell off balance and tumbled to the sidewalk. Mike laughed as he said, "You OK?" "I'm fine, you?" The tiny glimmer of light was enough for each of them to see the other's smirk. They both laughed. Mike stood first and offered his hand, "My lady." Patty took hold with one hand and pushed off the sidewalk with the other. "Yuck. Something gross got on my hand." Mike opened a flashlight app on his phone, revealing the blood on Patty's hand. They both looked down where they had fallen.

"Oh, crap!"

"Oh my god! Call 911."

Chapter 38 – Innocent

"What do you want from me?" Alice whined, to herself; and to the noise that echoed in her head. It was like little whispers taunting her. *Get to work Alice. He's mine, not yours. Robert is mature. We needed a man, not a boy. Be strong. It was an accident.* Alice planned to pen, as she liked to call it, a few words before calling it a night. It had been an exhausting day between the morning interview with the Monticello police and a trying afternoon at Jeff's funeral. Alice completely understood the Donovan family's animosity toward her. After all, they really did not know her. She did have a reputation for being a tad on the unstable side. Their younger son, Eric's brother, was dead. Murdered in cold blood. She tried to concentrate. Much of her writing came from real life events. She had no choice but to draw from all her experiences; even the sad and difficult ones. As Alice typed, her mind played tricks on her. She replayed Jeff's death in her head. She wrote of the passionate lovemaking turned rough sex. She saw his beautiful head hit the rocks; and blood oozing across them. She watched as her mind played out the fantasy turned horror. Jeff's blood rolled off the rocks and into the crystal-clear water. *It was an accident!* Alice jumped out of her chair. In front of her, on the computer screen, was the whole story. If it were truly fiction, it would be a winner. But, it was not fiction; it was a confession. "It wasn't an accident! You killed him!" *I fucked him; like you should have! It was an accident.* "Shut up! Shut up!" Alice sat on the floor crying. "Why are you in my head?" *I am you, my sister. And, you are I. You are my calm and I am the life you should be living. Let me out. Let me out*! "What do you want from me?" *I want to be you, I can give you peace, let me be in control. We can both be happy. You can take a break. It's like being in heaven. Just relax, don't fight me anymore.* "No. Shut up!" Alice stood up and ran into the bathroom to splash cold water on her face. She now, with all certainty, accepted that she was having a mental breakdown. "I'm going back to the doctors. I'm going to get help. Jeff was going to help me, but you messed that all up!" *Jeff was going to screw it all up for both of us. You may be done with Robert but I'm not.* "Robert is still mine!" *Robert is still mine!*

Alice screamed aloud for no one to hear, but she and her other self. The word processor, her ghost machine as she occasionally dubbed it for her own amusement, displayed the last words she had typed. Page after page magically disappeared until she focused on her right hand pressing "back space" on the keyboard, and released it. Alice wiped her nose with her sleeve, kicked off her shoes and headed for bed. A chill came over her, and she began to shiver. Alice pulled the comforter over her head and curled into a fetal position. How would she present all this to the doctors? She did not want to be in a hospital for crazy people, and locked up like a criminal. In truth, she thought, "I must be crazy. I may have killed someone I loved, and I just spent the evening arguing with a voice in my head." Alice had no one to talk with, and no one to console her. Robert had suddenly become a stranger. He had an entire other life that did not include her. Her mom would likely insist she commit herself to a mental health facility, and her daughter hardly knew her. The voice in her head was the only entity that understood her.

"I hate you, Robert."

I can get him back for both of us.

****

Detective Johnson originally planned to return downstate after her meeting in Monticello, but decided to stay overnight and poke around the crime scene on Friday morning. After the funeral ended, she walked over to Sergeant O'Malley, who was there to pay his respects. He invited her to join him and his wife for dinner that evening. Detective Johnson explained that she wanted to run surveillance overnight at Beekman's lake house. The

Sergeant offered to have one of his men watch the house for the first part of the evening, while they had dinner. He added, "This will give us a chance to talk more about our case, and yours. Maybe we can help each other." Rhonda gratefully accepted.

With no hotel stay planned, Rhonda headed over to the lake house. She drove past the house, noting the one car in the driveway belonging to Alice. Rhonda stopped about 300 feet up the road, and parked with an unobstructed view of the house. She reached into her cooler bag taking out half of a tuna sandwich. She took a bite and reached for her thermos of coffee. She sighed and mumbled to herself,

"It's going to be a long night."

As prearranged, an officer rolled up at exactly 6:30PM. Rhonda thanked him and promised to relieve him in a few hours. She drove off to meet O'Malley and his wife.

The conversation was light and friendly. Mrs. O'Malley proudly displayed several family photos of her and her husband with their daughters, on her iPhone. *Saved by the ring.* Rhonda apologized as she pulled her phone out of her pocket. She saw the caller ID, and excused herself. On the other end of the line, Detective Bill Reynolds said,

"You want the bad news or the good news first?" Rhonda replied, "Bad first." Bill cleared his throat.

"OK, so we had another homicide. Same M.O. Definitely our guy, or more likely gal."
"Crap! Where this time?"
"Last night, here in West Hartford."

"I tried calling you earlier but your phone didn't even seem to ring. I figured you might be in a *dead* zone. Anyway, it seems that our killer is focused more on staying local on Hartford turf. Not that I'm complaining. So, what's the good news?"

"Our vic is alive! The killer left her for dead. Some kids found her and called 911. She had barely minutes left to live. EMT's were the first responders. They performed a miracle, and saved her." Rhonda asked, "And the kids; did they witness anything?" Bill sighed, "Nah. They didn't see or hear anything. We think they happened upon the victim about five minutes after the attack. They were pretty shaken up." A moment of silence passed before Rhonda remarked, "It's a good thing they didn't run into the monster; that would have been bad." Bill agreed, "I suppose."

Rhonda became optimistic, her unsub had become careless. The case had been dormant for three years.

Finally, this woman might be the break they needed. Detective Reynolds went on to describe the victim's account of what happened. "Our very lucky young lady, her name is Janice, expressed her gut feeling that the attacker was female." Bill continued to tell Rhonda, "From the amount of blood, we can assume our killer now has a nice big scar somewhere on her face. Likely below one of her ears, or possibly, below an eye. We are waiting for DNA analysis to come back, but I'm certain it will be a match."

Rhonda hung up with Bill Reynolds and returned to her associate and his wife. "I'm so sorry; work. I'm sure you understand." Mrs. O'Malley laughed, "Sure do; don't we hun?" They finished their coffee, and said good night. "Thank you both for a pleasant evening. I'm going to go and relieve your officer now. Please let me know if anything else turns up that further incriminates Miss Beekman." They all stood up to leave. Rhonda added, "I'm going to head home later this evening. I won't need to visit the crime scene tomorrow. I'll call you if something changes."

Rhonda stayed for a few moments after the local patrol officer drove away. She sat staring at the mostly dark home of her *person of interest*. She considered how peaceful and quiet it was and thought to herself, "How nice to have a place up here." She said out loud, "Oh well, perhaps someday." The officer she just relieved had confirmed that no one came or left the home while he was on watch. He also noted movement in the house and lights going on and off indicating someone's presence. Disappointed at such a waste of her time, Rhonda headed back to the city. Her mind worked hard as she drove. She figured that this new information pretty much cleared Alice Beekman for the serial kills. But then again, the Donovan murder is still unsolved. Alice could be guilty of that one kill, or the serial killer found her way to the lake region. Alice was not off all the lists; at least, not yet. Then to herself she said, "She's the local yokel's problem."

Chapter 39 – Reflections of me

"Damn." Alice re-read the last few paragraphs at least three times, making changes to clarify the story for her readers. Her current quandary created an abundance of stress, causing her mind to play tricks on her. Alice's ability to concentrate on her writing was difficult. Writing had always come easy to Alice. Ideas flowed from her head to paper as fluidly as if she had predetermined the content. This was the first book, professionally, where she experienced writer's block more often than not. Yet, at times, it seemed as if the book wrote itself.

Frustration and fatigue plagued Alice, in both body and soul. Because of the agonizing stress she had to endure, depression was inevitable. This Molotov cocktail of emotions caused her many sleepless nights, which resulted in intensifying all the bad issues surrounding her. Sadness hung over her like a storm cloud ready to let loose on the earth below. Alice got up from her more than perfect workspace and stretched. She raised her hands high above her head, "Ooh, Ah. That feels a little better." After a quick gaze at the lake, Alice did an about-face and made her way to the bedroom. She knew she had to get over her paranoia. The signs accusing her of horrible things and the trespassers on her property unnerved her.

Every time she looked down along the shore, she imagined herself and Jeff walking, hand in hand. The sensitive memory always ended up turning ugly. Jeff would turn to kiss her. His lips were soft and delicious. She almost melted as the heat of his tongue gently and passionately brushed her lips. She saw herself repeatedly on top of him. They were making love, just as the old woman told the detectives and the news media. Her heart would pound as she envisioned Jeff lying bloody, broken, and alone on the rocky shore. It never dawned on Alice that Jeff's body was discovered floating in the lake. Pieces of the puzzle were often missing, and her vision of events were grossly distorted. Things that may, or may not, have happened to her or those close to her. She felt so empty and alone. "Oh Alice, what am I going to do with you?" Sitting on the edge of her bed, Alice stared into the full-length mirror mounted on her closet door. She waited for an answer. "Sure, when I need someone to talk to, you give me the silent treatment." Her eyelids grew heavy; she needed a nap. "Crazy person; now you're talking to yourself." As she looked at the reflection of herself, she envisioned the way she looked that night after Rob's company party in the city. She remembered letting go of her inhibitions. She had fun. That sensation she fought so hard against, now plagued her. She was ashamed, but in truth, she wanted to be that person again.

Alice curled up into a fetal position and quickly fell into a coma-like sleep. Dreams came to her, sometimes in a sleep state, and other times as daydreams. So often, they seemed real. Many times, her dreams would end up as written words on her computer; words she had no recall of authoring.

Alice skipped her way across an open green field. In front of her, was a child dancing and skipping. Her long blond hair trailed behind her like a kite's tail in the wind. Her daughter stopped and turned to face her with a huge smile. Then, as if someone else called the child's name, she turned and raised her arms.

The stunning, happy mother lifted her little girl high into the air. Alice stood still, watching as her doppelganger held the child and kissed her forehead.

Clouds formed and the beautiful green field lost all of its color. Her dream went black and white. The child shed tears of loneliness and abandonment. Her other self, spoke. The words echoed loudly in her head as though she was in a tunnel. "This is no child of yours. I conceived her! That is why you could never bond with her. You never wanted her. You need to let me out."

"LET ME OUT!"

Alice jumped in her sleep as her sister shrieked those last words; then awoke on the floor. Alice cried aloud, "You didn't want her. I don't remember making her." Her arm hurt really badly from the fall. Tears formed, as they seemed to do on a daily basis. Alice sat up and leaned her back against the side of her bed. The floor was hard on her bottom but it did not matter. Nothing mattered at the moment. She closed her eyes.

You win. Tell me what you want so I can have peace. Sarah said, *I want a life in the open. I want Robert. I want my daughter.* Alice finally became aware of her other self. *But we are the same. Our minds are one. If she is your daughter, then she is mine too. If you get Robert back, then so do I.*

No!

As if roles changed, Alice now recognized she lived two distinct lives from her one physical self. Sarah on the other hand now wanted it all for herself.

I will not let you bury me away like a turd in the backyard, Sarah.

So, Alice. You're aware of me? Awesome! Only one of us can drive this Ferrari of a body. You've seen me in action, felt what I felt. I'm the one having great sex with both of them. Well, one of them now. Sorry about that. It was me whose body quivered over and over in ecstasy. I did all the work and got all the pleasure. You experienced what little satisfaction was left over after the fact. You didn't even know what had happened to you. Face it. I've always been aware of you. I took what I wanted when I wanted, and when I was done, I let you back into the picture. Cruel and selfish wins the race. Look at me. Look at me!

Alice opened her eyes and looked at herself in the mirror, only to see her other self, smiling back. She was well aware that there was no smile on her face.

"Stop it! I changed my mind. I don't want to hear you."

Stop it! Stop it! Stop it. Stop. But, you know it's true. I'm the one he wants.

The last words echoed into silence. Sarah was gone; for now.

Chapter 40 – Ultimatum

The crowd at Rocka Rolla jumped up and down to the blaring music. Williamsburg's hottest nightspot lived up to its reputation. Robert found the one unoccupied stool at the crowded bar. He called Williamsburg Brooklyn his home for the past two years. He had needed an easier commute to his Manhattan office. From his former residence in Glendale Queens, it took him more than ninety minutes between driving to the railroad, and then taking the subway downtown. After weeks of painstaking searching, Alice found this apartment for him. She boasted, "It's only five subway stops to your office and a few blocks to walk. And, you're only ten minutes from me." It did work out well. Now, his complicated relationship with her and her sister really messed him up. Sarah was like a drug. Her spontaneity and sassiness made his body aware of sensations he never knew existed. He had to have her, regardless of the consequences. Yet, Alice was even-keeled and predictable. She was drop dead gorgeous. They both were. After all, they were identical twins.

"What's your flavor, boss?" The bartender's inquiry snapped Rob back to the here and now. He looked behind the server at the eclectic assortment of beer choices. "Let's go with the Woodchuck Amber." With a smile, the bartender nodded, "Good choice."

The young woman to Rob's left laughed loudly. She then bumped shoulders with him. He turned toward her, but she made no attempt at an apology. She was too engrossed in conversation with a few of her friends standing around her, and perhaps a tad over the edge drunk. The bartender placed Rob's beer in front of him. "Can I get you anything else? How about an appetizer?" Rob said, "No thanks. I'm good." The bartender snatched up a crumbled napkin left by the previous customer. "Enjoy."

The beer had a unique, crisp and delicious, flavor; Rob liked it a lot. He planned to try another of the local brews and play his own comparison game. He had chosen this place earlier after speaking to Sarah who told him she needed to see him right away. He really wanted a mellow night with no pressure and no sex. He wasn't sure about the latter and assumed that if Sarah showed up, sex was inevitable.

Sarah left Alice at home, metaphysically; allowing her to be in control for the moment. Now that Alice became somewhat aware of her, she had to be careful of what she said or did. As part of her playful and partially cruel intentions, Sarah called Robert's cell phone while standing on Metropolitan Avenue, just outside the bar. She wondered how the idiot never questioned why her phone had caller ID blocked. Or, why Alice's phone had the same. She was still angry with him and his Hartford based infidelity. Robert's phone vibrated just as he took a healthy swig of his brew. "Ok. Ok." He pulled his phone from the inside pocket of his sport jacket. "Robert here."

"Hey, what's going on?"
"Alice?"
"Yes. Who else would call you this late? Certainly not a client."
"Hey, babe. How are you? Things calming down at all?"
"Oh, you're concerned are you? Difficult to tell since you haven't called me. Anyway, I'm sorry we fought. Where are you? It sounds noisy."
"I stopped for a beer. Needed to ease off the day."
"So, Robert; I thought I might pop on by. See if we can mend a few fences. You do want to clear the air, don't you?"
"Oh, sure. But I thought you were upstate."
"I'm driving down now; about an hour out. Are you at Rocka Rolla? Sounds like the place is hopping tonight."
"I am, Alice. Babe, I'm out of here in a few. Really tired from a rough day. Can we do breakfast in the morning, early?"
"I planned to come down to see you tonight. You've

been unapproachable more and more or traveling to see her; I mean that client in Hartford. I have to be back upstate tomorrow first thing. You know; the whole mess. And, my publisher is freaking out."

"I'm sorry, babe..."

Sarah, posing as Alice was not letting him off easy. How rude he was.

"No problem. I guess I can turn around and head back to the lake. Thanks a lot. I guess you really care about me."

Silence. "Unknown Caller" now showed as "Call Ended."

The guilt seed planted, she was now ready for the next phase of the game.

Robert signaled the bartender for another. "Let's try that one." He pointed. The server nodded as he said, "Another good choice." Rob's hands were a bit shaky from nerves. He thought, *what if Alice decides to come, anyway. What if the two of them run into each other here at the bar, tonight? That would be the end all for me.* Rob guzzled half his beverage.

"Guess who!" For a split second, his heart stopped as soft hands covered his eyes and equally soft lips lightly pecked his neck. At first, he thought it was Alice, and his heart skipped a beat. He quickly regained his composure, realizing it had to be Sarah. Besides, her hands smelled of lavender; Sarah's signature fragrance.

"What are we drinking handsome?" Sarah leaned into Rob and with one hand took hold of his beer for a taste. Her other hand found his inner thigh, teasing his senses. The bartender asked, "Can I get you something, Miss?" Sarah, her left hand still holding Rob's leg hostage, put down the beer. "This 'Miss' needs something more serious. I'll have a vodka martini, dry, with three olives." She winked flirtatiously at the bartender, "Fill it to the brim." He glanced at Robert and then nodded to Sarah. Robert fought off the jealousy. The guy behind the counter wasn't the only one to be smitten with his little trollop. Besides, Sarah would never deal with that kind of emotional crap.

"You look incredible tonight. I've missed you." Sarah slid her hand upward, and then removed it abruptly. "I bet you say that to her, too. After all, she looks just like me. We are the same, aren't we? But, you do prefer me to her. Tell me the truth." Robert hated when she did this. He was well aware of her taunting games. "What would you do if *she* were to walk in right now and see us together?" Robert asked, "Why would you even ask that?" Rob suddenly felt butterflies taking flight in his stomach. He asked again, "Why would you think that might happen?" "Because, Robert, my love; it could.

215

What if she wanted to see you and decided to drive downstate? It would be an ugly scene. For you and her; but not me. I'm already on board about you and her. *Not really*. But, if she found us here together, you would have to make a decision on the spot. Me or her. Me or her!" The people to his left looked up for a second before going back to their engrossing banter. In a softer, almost sexy voice, "Me or her; Robert. What would you do?" Sarah placed her hand back on his thigh, a fraction of an inch from his bulging manhood. "You, Sarah! Damn it; you!" He kissed her hard. Her tongue found his while engaging in a sensual battle for control. The rude girl, now annoyed at Rob's back pressing against hers said, "Really? Why don't you two get a room?"

Rob tossed two twenties on the bar as he whispered into his neighbor's ear, "Thanks for the good advice." He took Sarah's hand, leading her outside to the street. "Let's go to your apartment." Rob had never asked about her apartment or anything about where she actually lived. They always ended up at his place. "We can't do that. Besides, you live two minutes from here, and I can't wait any longer than that." She took the lead, guiding him down Metropolitan. "You're worried Alice might show up at your place? She is upstate, isn't she? Remember what you said. You choose me. Maybe if she knocked on your door, this charade would be over; finally.

216

We could be rid of Alice." As she said that, Sarah realized her real desire to be her and not Alice. But, she had nothing. She did not exist to anyone except Robert. As the two of them hurried toward Robert's apartment, they stopped several times, kissing passionately. His hands would find their way all over her body. She had to stop him each time to avoid drawing too much attention. Sarah smiled; she had it all. She could pose as Alice once Alice was gone. She would always know that Robert really chose her. Now, she would have to figure out how to make that scenario work. She loved a challenge.

After a night of lovemaking that would rival the best of any porno film, Robert found sleep at around 4 AM. The sun woke him at 5:45. Her scent of sex and lavender aroused him. He rolled over to find that he was alone. Sarah had left a note on her pillow.

"Good morning, lover. I told you I had to leave early. Lots to do over the next few days. I'll call you. Last night was incredible. Remember; I choose you, too."

Confused and horny, Robert sat up in bed. He looked around the room. She *was* gone. He never actually missed her before. Sarah was one point of the triangle of his romantic life. She was the icing on the cake. Alice always took priority over his infidelity. This morning, things were different. He wanted more of Sarah. All of her; all the time. This, he knew, was going to be a challenging feat to accomplish. He leaned back against his propped up pillows. Then it hit him. Sarah never told him *she* had to leave early. Alice, last night, on the phone, said she had to leave early to head back upstate. He had a similar strange feeling once before. As if they were one in the same, or they were both toying with him. Robert knew his only choice was to break it off with Alice. Besides, Alice had no time for him. Her writing always came first. Sarah somehow seemed to be available for him when Alice wasn't around. Although, he had to consider the strange disappearing acts. Where did she need to run off to so early in the morning? Before this morning, a wall between the two sisters kept guilt from haunting him. The affair with his client in Hartford meant nothing to him; it was *business with benefits*. The moment Robert admitted to himself that his desire for Sarah pushed Alice into second place; desire won the battle over guilt. Not so long ago, life rolled along in a smooth, forward facing direction. Now it zigzagged in an exciting but nerve-racking path.

Chapter 41 - Guilt

"Bye, bye Miss American Pie, drove my Chevy to the levy but the levy was dry.
And good old boys were drinking whiskey and rye.
Singing…"

Sarah sang along with Don McLean's musical lyrics as she exited the interstate. In her head, she heard an echo of the words. She continued singing; hoping it would help to keep her focused. She knew Alice, like a stalker in waiting, would soon fight to regain control. "Not today, my sister." Sarah noted that the time was 9:30 AM. Fortunately, traffic was lighter than usual, allowing her to make good time.

As she drove through town, the rumbling in her stomach suggested a breakfast stop at the town diner. Bacon, scrambled eggs, and lots of coffee seemed like a good idea. Sarah pulled into a parking spot directly in front of the restaurant.

No! We should go home.

"Sorry sister; Hunger prevails."

Alice planned to avoid public places for a while. None of these people were her friends. Friendly acquaintances, perhaps.

"Good morning, Tony." Sarah smiled at the establishment's owner. Alice had been eating meals, mostly breakfast at his place since she purchased the lake house. Tony had always been friendly. Today his just nodded and went back to reading his newspaper. Sarah was about to say something rude.

Don't!

Alice fought for control but Sarah continued to say her piece before letting go. "What's the matter, Tony? Is ignoring your favorite customers a new business strategy these days? Oh; perhaps the *sauce* got the better of you this morning?"

Sarah grinned before turning away and switching channels.

You are too nice and submissive. These people acted like your friends, now they frown at you. Screw them!

Alice ignored the annoying voice in her head and took a seat at the mostly vacant counter. *Order something delicious.* Her stomach still rumbling from hunger. The waitress working the other end of the counter called out, "Good morning, Miss." As the server addressed her customer, she grabbed a menu from in front of another patron who sat quietly, minding his own business. She started walking over to Alice. Alice did not recognize the woman and figured she was a new employee. The waitress's face gave away her surprise at recognizing Alice from the news broadcasts. "Oh. You're Alice Beekman." She paused for a second; she appeared to have embarrassed herself. "Sorry. What can I get you?" Alice smiled, "I am, and I'll have the breakfast special, bacon crispy and coffee; please." The waitress took the menu that Alice handed to her, and returned with a hot cup of coffee. "The locals giving you a hard time?" Alice, happy for any friendly conversation said, "Some of them. They think I did something horrible to one of their own, but I didn't. He was my friend." "Listen, sweetie. They got nothing much going on in this sleepy town. You brought excitement into their dull lives. Only, they can't act like it's giving them something to do unless they can point fingers. I've seen you on TV. I haven't read any of your books yet, but I plan on picking one up this weekend. Would you please sign it for me the next time you come in for a meal?" She gave the sweetest *please, could you, smile*? Then she continued, "Besides, your predicament is probably good for business." Alice took a sip of her coffee. "My books are about sex and sometimes violence. After reading one of them, you might snub me too. You might think I'm acting out one of my stories." The waitress frowned. "Give me a little credit. I'm smarter than that. Your true friends, the people who count, will stand by you. The rest? To hell with them." She winked, "Let me get your breakfast before it gets cold."

Alice ate her breakfast in peace. The nice waitress brought her the check and said, "I bet they'll be sorry when the truth comes out. All this will settle down for you soon enough. You have yourself a really fine day, Miss Beekman." Alice smiled, "Thank you. Please call me Alice." Alice grabbed her handbag and headed toward the diner's main door. From behind her, she heard the waitress call out,

"Hey, Alice. Would you?" She hesitated then continued, "Sign your book for me?"

Alice looked over her shoulder smiling, "I'd be honored." She was not sure if the waitress really needed her to say yes to signing the book; or that she simply wanted to verbally flip off the less than empathetic patrons.

As Alice left the diner, she caught the owner, hard faced and covertly glancing her way. His expression changed as the sexy blond writer sneered at him and walked out of the restaurant.

Was that me, or you?

All you, Alice. All you.

Alice pulled into her driveway. As she got out of her car, she looked around for any more invasions of her privacy. There were no new tire tracks in the gravel. She walked down the hill along the side of her house. As far as she could see, there were no other signs naming her as a killer. She took a deep breath and exhaled. The lake looked so inviting, but she still could not bring herself to walk down to it. Alice thought, how nice and relaxing it would be to kayak along the shoreline. To herself she mumbled, "I'd have to buy one first." *Sure, and one of the power boaters might swamp you!* Alice had no time to argue with herself over such a trivial desire. She had much work to do in order to finish her book. The publisher's indulgence held up until now, thanks in part to her agent's intervention. However, their patience would soon wear thin. The delay allowed for a bit of free media hype to perk up interest about Alice as the author. They were certain curiosity would lead to increased book sales. Regardless, deadlines and planned publishing release dates had to be met or she could lose shelf space in the larger retail outlets. Her people did not have to tell her that too much of a delay might very well backfire, resulting in disappointed readers as well.

The house had an emptiness that added to Alice's depression. She missed Jeff, and needed Robert more than ever. "Next weekend I'll go see him; if he lets me.

223

Maybe we can work through our issues." As Alice said the words aloud to the empty house, Sarah responded to her from within her head. *Yes, we will work it out. He can have both of us. We need to be creative and put the pen to the paper, Alice.*

Hey! That's my line.

The writing unexpectedly flowed like a river after a torrential rainstorm. Page after page appeared in front of her. Alice stopped just as dusk fell upon the lake. The night lights from various homes along the shore started popping on, one by one. Little by little, sparkling reflections appeared on the water. It looked so beautiful. This was Alice's favorite time of day. Her book, near completion, needed a read-through before writing the final chapter. Alice clicked on the navigation side bar of her word processor and selected the chapter titled "Epilogue." She stared at the blank page for a moment, trying to imagine what verbiage should appear on the page. Alice flipped back a few chapters and started reading. After a while, she realized how closely the fictional story followed real life events. Her life! "Oh my god; this is almost incriminating." *It's just fiction, Alice.* Alice re-read one of the chapters as her heart ached.

He was in love with me, this I knew for sure. His eyes gave it away each time we were together. I never admitted to him how much I cared for him. He was my friend. We had sex, but never really made love. Although, I'm sure if he and I could have another discussion about our carnal time together, his perception would differ. He would say we made love. That final day of passion, the one I find so hard to recall, yet my body knows it happened, proved to me that I loved him. I would have given it all up for him. I know this now. But now, it's too late for us. Death has taken my true love from me.

Alice read the passage repeatedly, considering if she should remove it. Her finger rested on the "delete" key of her computer, but something prevented her from pressing down on it. An unexplainable and overpowering force controlled her hand. As she continued to read successive chapters, her guilt became more obvious. The names overtly changed but the actions and even more so, the emotions of the characters were all so real. Alice read on as if someone else had written about her life. She became light headed, Alice envisioned herself all made up, the way she looked on those occasions she found so very hard to recall. She barely recalled the party in New York City, but had vivid memories of how she overtly seduced Robert. It looked like her, but it was not her. She saw herself at the bar in Monticello talking to Jeff, seducing him that night and waking up in the morning, freaking out. Robert called her Sarah on more than one occasion. Jeff called her Alice. She considered her dilemma of two lovers. The one that wanted her to be someone else, and the one who loved her for who she was; even in her irrational moments. She had had options. Now only the one remained, and Robert was an unknown.

He cheated on us. He should beg us for forgiveness.

Alice looked down upon Jeff's face as she moved her body up and down on him. She could feel the ecstasy Sarah brought upon her and Jeff that final day. He seemed uncomfortable, and therefore not in control. When he was with Alice, Jeff was always in control. He offered stability and sensible actions. This was not her. It was this ugly soul, Sarah, who was stuck in her head. Alice, looking down upon herself and Jeff like an angel in the sky, now watched as blood flowed, covering the rocky bed, they had just had sex on. Sarah killed Jeff!

Alice snapped back to reality. She cried out for no one to hear. Confusion overwhelmed her. Was she living the fictional story, or was the story reliving her life as it happened?

Chapter 42 – Dream

Writing filled her day, making time pass quickly. For Alice, this was a blessing, as time represented reminiscing those too few happy moments she shared with her two lovers. Until now, she fooled herself into seeing Jeff as a friend with limited benefits. By the time she realized she wanted more from him, time had run out. Robert remained an unknown at this moment. He cheated on her with at least one other woman; that bitch of a client in Hartford, and she feared a second would turn up if she allowed his escapades to continue. Then again, he may be done with her after her admission to spending that one night with Jeff. Even under the bizarre circumstances of that night, Robert might never let it go.

Maybe we should call it even. He's a big boy. Time for him to pony up in the relationship and take ownership for his part of the problem.

Alice held her head between her hands so tightly, she thought she might crush it. "No! What he did was intentional and deceitful. Why don't you shut up?"

She sat on the edge of her bed, weeping from profound sadness. As the tears streamed down her cheeks, she reached over to the cute little nightstand she found at an antique fair a few months ago, and yanked a tissue from its box. Exhausted and frustrated, Alice had hoped that if she could fall asleep, perhaps god would be kind and take her peacefully.

Fortunately, for Alice, falling asleep never seemed to be an issue for her.

A little girl ran across the yard, her bare feet bouncing on the soft green grass. Her mother had the biggest smile as she opened her arms, inviting Alice to jump into them. As their eyes meet, her mom shifts to the right, a little. Alice watches as her mom hugs so tightly the cutest little child; a child that looked like her. Sadness filled her little soul as she stood and watched. She felt abandoned.

In her sleep, Alice called out, "Mommy, that's not me. I'm over here, Mommy."

A chilling breeze brought darkening skies. Mommy faded away and Alice now stood on a dark street. The street sign had letters, but they were unreadable. From afar, she heard the frenetic barking of a dog. The way its howling echoed, it must have been a good distance away; at least several blocks. Alice looked up and down the street, trying to get her bearings. She had no idea where or when she was, but the frequency of these occurrences made it seem almost natural. Something caught her eye, distracting Alice from her confused state of mind. Across the street a car is running, the car door on the passenger side is open. There is no movement. She does not remember walking over to the car; magically, she found herself transported across the street, onto the grassy apron of the sidewalk.

"Hello? Are you OK?" Alice again speaks aloud in her sleep. "Hey, you. Wake up!"

The young man appears to be sleeping; perhaps drunk and passed out. Alice moves closer to get a better look. She sees blood on his fingers. His eyes are wide open, but appear empty. His skin is so pale. She senses his soul is gone. Taken before its time. Alice considers the possibility that she is culpable for the horrific scene in front of her. She often skips bits of time and space. Panic approaches as she realizes that she may be the monster people believe she is. In the blink of an eye, she is back in her lake house. It is dark outside, but something down by the shoreline reflects light that catches her attention. It's a wooden sign made of old driftwood, staked into the ground. Written in freshly dripping blood, the sign reads, "Murderer! This Way" and points up toward where she is standing in the window.

"I couldn't have done it! I didn't mean to. I'm sorry, Jeff. I loved you."

Alice awoke abruptly in a cold sweat. She remembered the dream as if she had written it. Her stomach churned, and she cupped her hands, thinking she might vomit. Memories of other tortured bodies now sat somewhere in the back of her mind. She had no clear vision of them. She simply knew they existed.

Or, had her imagination gotten the best of her?

I am the author.

Chapter 43 – A day of reckoning

Over the next few days, Alice found herself moving in and out of reality more often than not. Her book continued to self-write chapter after chapter. Completion was nearing. She was both elated and relieved. The publisher's deadline for the final draft had been set for this Friday. Alice would have no problem meeting it, as it was only Wednesday, and she had completed the book's final chapter the previous evening. Alice tried to play the final chapters in her head, but could not. She laid back on her couch, placing a large puffy pillow behind her head. With her laptop resting on her stomach, she began to reread one more time.

Today, I became acutely aware of my other self. We are two complete souls sharing one body. One of us represents all the goodness real life can allow. The other, who I consider my nemesis, reveals herself as a free spirit, void of any inhibitions and with little empathy. I thought us to be separate, but now understand we cannot exist without each other. I represent complicity, remorse, respect and concern for others. My counterpart is everything I am not. If things went different, if that one tragedy had not occurred, all would be good. I fear for us now, as we are alone. I also fear that there are other things, evil things that Sarah has done, for which I am not consciously aware of. Images of death now haunt me. At first, the loss of my new best friend filled my heart with grief. Then with guilt. Lately, images of strangers, who I believe met an untimely demise, haunt me. I never see what happens to them. What I see is the cold emptiness in their eyes. If I said this to others, they might perceive me as more than crazy, perhaps completely insane; and before the most recent events that I am now aware of, it would have seemed so to me as well. But, I'm sure there is someone else. Another soul that has infiltrated my life. We've not communicated as Sarah and I do. This unknown entity sits outside our world. I fear she is the master who controls both Sarah and I. We are the puppets in her play. Evil surrounds me now. The reality of this world I thought I belonged in, leaves me with many questions. I tried calling my mother today. I wanted to hear her voice and that of our daughter, Grace. I tried several times, but the phone just rang and rang. I joke all the time saying, "I may be crazy, but I'm not nuts." Maybe I am nuts and there is no mother, no daughter. My memories may not be real. Grace may have represented my desire for normalcy, for family. Even Sarah; is she real? I never had a sister. Perhaps I made her up as a companion, or as an excuse to cheat and murder. Then, I have to also accept the possibility that I don't exist either. That third soul? Perhaps she is the only real person.

Alice stopped reading. She looked around her home. It appeared animated as if it were a made up prop created for use in a movie. A chill numbed her entire body. Nausea crept up quickly and disappeared just as fast at the abrupt banging on her front door.

Chapter 44 – The final chapter

The sun had set only moments ago; it was her favorite time of day. The earlier blue sky now had streaks of thin clouds, edged in red. Alice smiled in appreciation, knowing that in a moment, darkness would replace the mesmerizing view. One final look out of her window at the lake allowed her to observe the beginning of the shadowed reflections she found so beautiful. On the shore below, two people held hands as they kissed. She imagined it was Jeff kissing her. Oh, how she wanted to feel his strong and reassuring arms around her. He promised to help her, and to keep her safe. At this very moment, she was alone. She had never felt so abandoned.

Who's at my door? Said Alice...
It's the wolf, and I'm hungry! Open up or I'll huff, and I'll puff and then, I'll blow your house down!

The voice in her head completely lacked empathy as it giggled and faded away.

"Alice Beekman. We have a warrant to search your premises." The officer held up an official looking document in front of Alice. After five seconds, he folded the paper and put in his inside jacket pocket. She considered asking to read it, but something in the back of her mind said *don't bother*. Alice stood quietly, with no emotion. Where was Sarah now? "Am I under arrest?" The officer, wearing a state police uniform said, "Yes, Ma'am. I'm afraid so. Your downstate residence is also being searched at this time." The officer escorted her out of the house, her hands handcuffed behind her. Alice looked over her shoulder to see them bagging her laptop and various documents that were on her desk.

"That's my work; I have deadlines."

The officer eased Alice into the back of his dark brown police cruiser. He placed his hand over her head to prevent her from hitting it on the doorframe. *He seems nice; he is just doing his job*. From the patrol car's window, Alice took one last gaze at her beautiful lake house. She breathed in slowly through her nose, imagining the scent of the beautiful roses that lined her front porch.

Oh, how I remember falling in love with this home, at first sight.

Yes, sister. Its beauty even entranced me at times. I suppose I will miss the peacefulness of it as well.

As if in a dream, she imagined walking hand in hand with her sister among the rolling green hills and beautiful red Tulips. She had a moment of peace; then it all evaporated into thin air. Alice's brain seemed to be shorting out like a defective electrical circuit. She heard a voice in her head, but she had no idea who she was at the moment, or whose voice she was hearing.

"Your laptop and its contents are evidence now, Ma'am."

Alice heard the officer, but the words had no meaning any longer. Sarah wanted to call Robert. It was time to come clean. She hoped that he would come to her defense and explain to the police that *Alice* had killed Jeff. He could explain that Sarah was simply an innocent victim of the circumstance. Alice on the other hand, blamed herself for allowing Sarah to take control. She sat handcuffed in the back seat for what seemed like an eternity. Hours surely had passed. It had been dark for some time. With her eyes closed, Alice put her fears aside and took control.

My dear sister, I'm afraid we are going to do time together. I have wanted you out of my head for most of our torturous lives. Now I pray that you don't leave me alone. We can both pay for our sins by surviving. We can repent together for what you did, and for me not stopping you. I pray that a time comes when we can meld into one perfect human being.

Epilogue

"She had been speaking to me all my life, but I could not hear her. She somehow remained imperceptible to me, and from the rest of the world. I always considered myself crazy; never understanding that there were two of us in this one body. My sister. I'm sure, was always aware of me. Her frustration and loneliness can explain, while not justify, her sometimes cruel intentions. I was content. She was not. I was living life in the open, as me, while all she wanted was to be me; and her."

Christine Hanson read the excerpt with passion. This book signing, her first for the newly released thriller novel drew a substantial audience. The West Hartford bookstore hosting her book debut was one of the largest in the country. Her agent, as well as her literary team of editors, fact checkers, and marketing people, stood in various places on the outskirts of the crowded room. Jack Rosen, a representative from her publisher, stood next to her while they posed for pictures.

Back at the signing table, cameras panned to show ranks of devoted fans waiting to purchase copies of the novel. The line wrapped around three aisles. An equal number of fans waited patiently to have their copy personally signed by their favorite author. As an added bonus, Christine's agent had a personal connection to a local television news reporter, who agreed to cover the evening's event. "So, Miss Hanson, your latest novel, 'Becoming Alice' is flying off the shelves tonight. You must be very pleased." The author smiled as she wrote a message of thanks, and autographed another book. She paused for a moment to acknowledge her next fan. With the pen still in her hand, she responded to the interviewer as she had several times throughout the evening, "I am so very pleased with the turnout. I love my readers, and worked exhaustingly hard, to create a story that would meet with their expectations for a suspenseful romance plagued with tragedy. It's an old story remixed; don't you think?" The reporter said, "Like a twisted Romeo and Juliet?"

"To Alison, with sincere appreciation. Enjoy the read."

She handed the autographed book to the young girl telling her, "What a pretty name. I almost used it for my book. I'm going to use it in my next one." The girl smiled, "Thank you so much, Miss Hanson." The next person in line, a man of about forty, handed her his book. "I love your books, Miss Hanson. Please make it to Jimmy D." The author started writing and said, without looking up at her interviewer, "Well, not exactly like those two young lovers. However, the mix of sex and violence is a magnet for people who fundamentally live an 'honorable' life that ends in tragedy. My readers want the fantasy to cross extreme boundaries. Look around, ask anyone, or one hundred of them." Christine looked around the vast open area, still filled with people waiting for their fifteen seconds with her. The reporter glanced up at the camera for effect, and then back to his subject, "Just one more question. People are saying you ripped part of the story from the news headlines like that television show." After another pause, for effect, she sternly said, "My readers can identify better with the characters, if they simulate real life events. In truth, reality can be boring. That is where the creative fiction comes into play. I see it as a healthy mix." She looked around and gestured with a nod towards the crowd. "Apparently, it's effective. Don't you agree?" The reporter ignored the last statement and asked, "Some of the timelines, the characters, are a bit unbelievable. The boyfriend, Robert, what man has that kind of luck?" The reporter made a face that expressed, without words, "Well?"

"That's two."

"Two what?"

"You said, one more question, but asked me two."

The author grinned indicating she was busting chops on the reporter and continued. "Well, as I said earlier, it's fiction. The story allows the reader to make their own judgments... it allowed them to live the fantasy." The reporter put on a serious face, "They say the reality is never as good as the fantasy. Do you agree?" The interview was getting off track, and both parties seemed to be getting agitated. Christine reached for another book. "What's your name, sweetheart? I love your blouse. It's such a pretty color." The author signed her name and returned the book to her loyal fan. She then looked directly at the reporter, "I'm not so sure that is true in all cases." Her smile turned into a chilling grin. "I often place myself into the story. Think of it like a Broadway play where the writer is also the star of the show. I can write the fantasy, and then adlib it as the performance carries on. When I'm creating a story, it becomes my reality."

Or perhaps, it is reality that becomes my story.

****

Detective Stanley Barnes was a huge fan of Christine Hanson's books. He watched the live broadcast from his New York City home with his family. He paid close attention as the author read excerpts from her book. In fact, he had bought the book earlier in the week, just one day after it hit the shelves. After reading the first few chapters, Barnes found it fascinating how closely the story paralleled a real case he was working. An all-nighter allowed him to complete the read. Until seeing this televised interview, no direct connection between the author's story and his case clicked.

As the reporter asked questions and Christine Hanson responded, the detective felt his heart skip a beat. The camera caught an angle of the author's face where the light exposed what looked like a mark below her right ear that ran across and below her right eye. He moved closer to the television. "Dad, what are you doing?

You're blocking the TV!" Barnes stared at her face as it turned away, hiding what he thought could be a scar covered by makeup. Then it hit him like an avalanche. The detective in her story, Rhonda Johnson; that was him! He mumbled, "Really? You made me a woman?" His wife asked, "Are you OK, Hun?" He considered it crazy, but had to go with it, anyway. So much of the story fit, even though the names were changed. He also remembered from another interview with People Magazine, that Christine Hanson was a gym rat. She described her gym workouts, usually four days a week, as "intense." That explained how a woman could overpower her victims. Detective Barnes picked up his phone and made the call as he did three years earlier.

"West Hartford Police. What is your emergency?"

****

Never Alone

Christine Hanson noticed a commotion at the far end of the store. Men in suits, followed by what appeared to be soldiers, slowly made their way around the perimeter. She turned to see the alarmed look on her agent's face. The TV cameras diverted their focus to the commotion. "Crap. You think someone made a bomb threat or something?" Christine shook her head, but said nothing in response to his concern. She knew why they were there. The men in suits were detectives. The soldiers were members of the swat team.

West Hartford police managed to get a warrant to search the author's residence. A preliminary DNA test taken from evidence found in her home was a direct match to all the victims logged over the years.

What do you want to do today?

"What I do every day, all day."

Exercise, exercise. Enough!

"Never enough, I need to keep active or I'll go crazy."

You are crazy; we are crazy.

"This is all your fault; I hate you."

I love you.

"These walls seem to close in more each day, I need space. I need a way to relieve this anxiety."

Her mind replayed all the lives she took; the life she squeezed out of them. She experienced a moment of pure elation.

"You; if I had gotten rid of you, none of this would have happened."

You can't get rid of me, I am you.

"I hate you Sarah!"

Sarah? Who is Sarah? She's a character you made up in your head – for a stupid story!

The pounding on the cell door echoed as it did each of the two times a day, meals were delivered. "Mealtime, princess." The guard placed the tray of sloppy Joe over mashed potatoes on the doors pass-thru shelf and waited. "Hey, you got till a count of ten to come get it before I take it away." Christine sat on the floor in the far corner of the room, staring into space. *The soft grass felt good on her bare feet. Oh how beautiful the red tulips were as they swayed in the gentle breeze. Which path should she take? There's always a choice.* The guard waited the ten seconds before saying, "Ok Alice, or whoever you are today; I warned you. Your ten seconds are up!" The guard waited a few more seconds in silence, and then removed the tray.

"Take my hand and walk with me."

"You are so beautiful."

"I am beautiful because of you. I look like you. We all do."

****

The alarm rang out loudly as swarms of prison guards and other personnel ran to Cell Block 13. The warden angrily asked, "What the hell happened? Who strangled her?" The prison doctor, who was in the middle of examining the dead author, stood up, shaking his head in wonderment. "She killed herself. Likely during a psychotic episode of extreme rage. One of her personalities tried to strangle the other. Obviously, one could not possibly commit suicide using that method as they would black out from the body's first mechanism of defense. Apparently, there's trauma to the top of her head. I think a broken neck is the cause of death." The warden asked, "How is that possible?" One of the guards spoke up, "She was a powerful woman, and super crazy." He pointed to the far corner of the room, gesturing to a small amount of blood splatter on the wall. "She bolted head first into the cinderblock." He pointed to the other end of the small room. "I guess she got lucky."

The warden turned, and made his way toward the door.

"I guess she did. Someone else will have to write the ending; to her story."

-   End   -

Note from the Author:

To all my faithful readers, thank you for your positive comments and support. I hope you have enjoyed reading my fifth novel, "Becoming Alice."

I welcome and encourage my readers to comment on my books and ask questions, especially, if clarity is needed for any part of the story. The best way is to visit my website

Please visit www.waynelasnerbooks.com for updates on all available books as they become available. Visit www.Amazon.com and search for Wayne Lasner to see all my published works.

Any mention of named characters are fictional and not based on real people. Like any fictional story, any depiction of social or religious beliefs are for entertainment and have no real bearing on the authors or publisher's political views.

Acknowledgement

I write fiction because I love to create a story that pushes the reader's imagination. While creating the story and putting it to paper takes a good deal of effort and time, the real work is in the editing.

I would like to thank all my friends and family for your continued support. To all of you who have read my books, it is your positive feedback that drives me to continue the creative process.

A special thank you to my editor Mark Goodman for your relentless efforts and patience and for your true dedication to the final product. Your life experiences in Military and Law Enforcement along with the love of fiction is what ensures that everyone else can truly enjoy a realistic, easy, and clear read.

Other Books by Wayne Lasner

The Jack Owens Series

    The Twin
    Rage
    True Deception

Crossing America

Available in Paperback and for Kindle at
Amazon.com